PRAISE FOR
RUPERT WONG

"Madcap, macabre and violently funny, with metaphor-rich, sensual prose. The more creative descriptions of gore pull the tale somewhere into the interstitial space between urban fantasy and horror, but brave readers will be richly rewarded if they choose to follow. It's probably safe."

N. K. Jemisin, *The New York Times*

"She's too good a writer to ignore."

Chuck Wendig

"Tight, tense, well-constructed urban fantasy… Khaw writes with vivid energy. Rupert's cynical and irreverent voice as a narrator is immensely appealing, and Rupert himself is a compelling character: aware that his residual morals sometimes make him a hypocrite, and more wearily resigned than shocked at every new horror that intrudes into his life."

Liz Bourke, *Locus*

"Even as the plot winds and turns and—from time to time—explodes, Rupert's unerring voice, expertly erudite and cleverly craven, serves as a homing beacon. At times, the chaos that envelops him can be confusing, but you forgive the messiness because, well, you just *like* Rupert. He's a well-meaning con, a courageous coward you can root for."

Barnes & Noble Sci-Fi & Fantasy Blog

"A gut-punch of a reading experience that swings the reader disturbingly between laughing out loud and beginning to retch. Descriptive imagery dances viscerally on the edge between the delicious and the disgusting; clever wordplay twines with heavy profanity; the mood flips rapidly among comedy, horror, and tenderness. This amazing book is perfect for foodies, readers of modernized mythology and light supernaturals, and fans of the smart, underpowered survivor who wins in the face of cosmic might and mundane brawn."

Publishers Weekly **Starred Review**

"Speaking of fun... a high-octane fantasy and murder mystery. It's got a near-perfect first chapter, and I'd love to see more in that world."

Lavie Tidhar

"Khaw is always tip-toeing the line between 'Oh, god, this is too much' and 'My stomach's churning, but in sort of a good way.' The underworld that Rupert travels through is degenerate and horrifying, but it's also creative and endlessly diverse. Despite the subject matter that pervades most of the book, it's *fun* to spend time with Rupert."

Tor.com

"*Rupert Wong, Cannibal Chef* is one of those books that you have to pick up when you find it, if only to see whether or not the title is screwing with you. Bottom line: if you can handle the profanity and grotesque content, you just may find this one to your liking..."

Manhattan Book Review

"This book is delicious fare, what fantasy is supposed to be. If you find it in a bookshop near you pick it up, devour it. After all, 'meat is meat.'"

Bosphorus Review of Books

"My favorite urban fantasy this year... Very fun, fast, quick read, and the protagonist's voice amused me."

Silvia Moreno-Garcia

"Rupert Wong is an engaging smartass of a character you can't help rooting for... Khaw's voice is needed in our discussions of genre and myth, and I look forward to what she comes up with next."

The Future Fire

"I honestly chuckled out loud a couple of times— something that rarely happens—and Rupert's voice is both irreverent and witty, a delightful mix... and a great sense of pacing."

The Middle Shelf

"The melange of different ideas of and approaches to divinity is reminiscent of Terry Pratchett's *Small Gods* and *Hogfather*, but Khaw takes it in a different, stranger, and altogether darker direction than simply a discussion of faith and reality; there's more of an interest in what faith *is*, and she engages with that quite fascinatingly."

Intellectus Speculativus

"Refuses to let Rupert off the hook, refuses to let him be the hero riding in on a silver horse. It fits, and it unsettles in a way that I think is important."

Quick Sip Reviews

An Abaddon Books™ Publication
www.abaddonbooks.com
abaddon@rebellion.co.uk

First published in 2019 by Abaddon Books™,
Rebellion Publishing Limited, Riverside House,
Osney Mead, Oxford, OX2 0ES, UK.

10 9 8 7 6 5 4 3 2 1

Creative Director and CEO: Jason Kingsley
Chief Technical Officer: Chris Kingsley
Head of Books and Comics Publishing: Ben Smith
Editors: David Moore, Michael Rowley and Kate Coe
Marketing and PR: Remy Njambi
Design: Sam Gretton, Oz Osborne and Gemma Sheldrake
Cover: Sam Gretton

ISBN: 978-1-78108-645-2

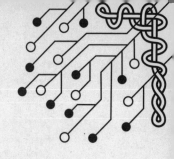

THE LAST SUPPER BEFORE RAGNAROK

CASSANDRA KHAW

ABADDON
BOOKS

For my editor, David Moore
Thank you for always believing in me.

ONE

MY NAME IS Rupert Wong.

If you're reading this, I assume you already know who I am. That or you're some terrifying otherworldly being, capable of overpowering Amanda and commandeering her private files, in which case I hope you find this account of recent events hilarious and adequate reason to abstain from devouring me. Of course, you could also be a teenage genius who accidentally broke into Amanda's folder, which seems strangely more plausible than the other thing.

In any event, regardless of which category you might fall in, I guess it wouldn't hurt to start with the basics:

Gods are real. Angels are real. The bushy-bearded pixies who fix your shoes for a thimble of milk? Also real and incredibly gung-ho about standardising labour laws. Same goes for the weird shit that you see on YouTube. That cat with the human hands. Horrifically, traumatically real.

There are several reasons as to why this information isn't as widespread as it could be. Chiefly, most of the entities that I've mentioned are unfeeling assholes who either kill or transform any human beings they encounter into gibbering wrecks. More often than not, they do both, and with no small amount of gusto. Gossip is hard when you're dead.

The other reason is a simpler one. Humanity, as a species, we don't do particularly well with being pushed outside of our comfort zone. We'd much rather scream, faint, laugh it away as banging on the pipes, block it out of our memory.

Between those two factors, the schism between what is and what people believe was inevitable. Which is okay. Because I like the idea of civilizsation being able to get up in the morning, make its coffee, and continue doing the things necessary for TV, adequate cuisine, and public transportation.

But I'm getting sidetracked.

As mentioned previously, my name is Rupert Wong. As was not mentioned previously, I die twenty-six times over the course of this book. And no, I don't mean this metaphorically, or poetically, or any of those other adverbs that suggest flower wreaths, people in nice suits, and a mid-tier buffet with a few canapés, and a bottle of discount prosecco. When your name is Rupert Wong, you die messily. Then, you get resurrected. Then, you die again.

Screaming.

A lot.

Anyway. This forward is intended to be a public service announcement. There will be chapters that feature events that I cannot possibly have knowledge of, but will have discussed very thoroughly. There's a small chance they could be fabrication. It depends entirely on Amanda, who will have supplied the material by virtue of having access to every piece of surveillance equipment known to mankind. Sometimes, Amanda likes being funny[1]. By and large, however, you should assume that the accounts are true albeit dramatised and react accordingly.

Or something.

Anyway, let's start—

* * *

"Like I said, I think I need you to help me save the world."

I look him over and glance sidelong at my plate of indomee goreng, the slab of fried egg with its yolk freshly split, and my glass of Milo, already sweating condensation onto the table.

"Can I say no?"

"No."

I consider my options. "In that case, I really need you to help me kill that dragon."

Fitz, to my surprise, doesn't look remotely perturbed. He shrugs, a smile gashes his face apart and he turns, almost like clockwork, towards the direction of the incoming Ao Qin. Bravery comes easy to those with no clue as to their limitations, I guess. That, or Fitz is certifiably delusional. I twirl a fork through my noodles and cram a mouthful into my face. Given my luck, this might be the only bite I get.

"He's a god, right?"

"Yeah."

"Oceanic?"

"Yup."

"Is his worship a common thing around here?"

"I have no fucking clue. Maybe? We've got that Dragon Boat festival thing, and—"

He nods. "I can work with that."

Guan Yin, let me one day have the confidence of a

white man who sees dragons as mere inconveniences. Fitz extracts an iPhone 8 from a pocket, its display spiderwebbed with cracks. I spear my fried egg as he pulls up Twitter, Facebook, Snapchat, Instagram, Weibo, every incarnation of social media known to the masses, all accessed through a third-party program I do not recognize. Likely because I suck at keeping up with the times, being both old and frequently preoccupied with the Herculean task of staying alive.

"What the fuck are you doing?" I mumble through a lot of egg.

"I'm going to fucking pontificate that lizard out of existence."

"What?"

Fitz doesn't answer. Instead, he reads into his phone, his voice taking on the rhythm of a sermon, low and rich and droning. Power shimmers through the air, jitters under my skin like static, close as a shave. It feels like a low-level electrocution. It feels like grace, like being threaded through the eyelet of fate. I don't immediately grok what he's saying, or the paeans he's reciting, but when I do, I'm a little flabbergasted by the venom. Fritz is recounting a death that Ao Qin has yet to suffer, and it's ugly.

What Fitz reads him is a small death, a death of being forgotten, of being mortal and unremarkable, of starving under a heat lamp in a college student's dormitory. A *pet's* death. When finally he is done, Fitz looks up, clears his throat again and hits *send*.

"There."

We wait.

I guzzle down half my Milo, faintly optimistic about my chances at making this an adequate last meal. Ao Qin, to no one's surprise, is in no hurry at all. A storm brews and ripples; I can hear the dragon god whisper, clacking promises, descriptions of deaths so lurid they'd make a serial killer blush. But he's not here yet. That's the important thing. The reptile likes an entrance, and far be it from me to look a gift dragon in the teeth.

"Any minute now." Fitz taps his foot on the asphalt.

We keep waiting.

"Any second." A frown collects between his feathery eyebrows. I finish my Milo and order another. No reason not to gorge at the unnatural end of one's lifespan.

The seconds continue to tick by.

"Hm," says Fitz.

"Hm?"

He examines his phone. "This usually doesn't take so long."

"No?" I can absolutely put away another plate of indomee. Feeling ambitious, I flag down a waiter, place a request for an indomee double, this time with fried chicken. As an afterthought, I add a teh tarik to go for my new acquaintance. "Yeah, I guess that was obvious. You looked… prepared for something more instantaneous?"

"Which it normally is."

"Mhm."

"…I'm not sure what's wrong."

"It's alright. It happens to everyone, sometimes."

Fitz spears me with an irritated look, but his vexation soon melts away, absents itself in favour of well-modulated terror. Without announcement, he crumples onto a plastic stool, a puppy-dog expression of loss grooved into his long, cocaine-wrung face. "I don't understand."

"I think, and I say this as someone who has no idea what the fuck you are, that this might be what you'd call an issue of East-versus-West. Now, I assume what you were trying to do is, uh, *talk* Ao Qin out of existence?"

"Yeah. Not the first time I'd done it, either. It works. Religions are defined by their prophets."

The waiter arrives with my order, and a plastic bag filled with milky taupe tea. I offer the latter to Fitz, who takes it quizzically.

"What the fuck is this?"

"Teh tarik. Anyway." I set my fork down. "I think the problem here is that you think that belief powers everything. Which it does, to an extent. But Southeast Asia is… special. We don't necessarily believe in one pantheon. We don't even always *believe*, I guess. We just… know they're there. The gods are carved into the grain of our souls, them and every cryptid in the wet tropical dark. They just *exist*. A thousand variations of them. All at the same time. And an ang moh shouting his concept of what's real is going to get nothing more than a shrug."

"Oh."

"Yeah."

"Shit. Time for Plan B, I guess."

"Okay, that sounds good. Any idea what that's gonna be?"

"I'm going to the Internet for help."

"*Right.*"

THERE ARE PLACES, ang moh, where the mountains move and no one looks up, because there's always a chance that they're coming for *you*. Reality bends in these cities, gyres along the fulcrum of minding-my-own-fucking-business, shears sidelong and away so the divine and the demonic can enjoy their gladiatorial encounters, all without needing to endure the stigma of being improbably mythological.

Which is probably why no one else has taken notice

of the flotilla of helicopters arrowing towards us. Then again, they might just be busy ignoring the dragon still hurtling our way.

"So. Let me get this straight." I look over at my new friend, who has since discovered one of Malaysia's most pragmatic inventions: the iced drink in a plastic bag. No fuss, no pretence, just a straw jabbed through one corner and a loop of pink plastic to keep it together. If only life was so easily parcelled. "Amanda just wants us to wait here. Does she actually have a plan?"

"She usually does." Fitz cocks his head like a dog listening for the buzzsaw whine of a can opener, mouth rucked. The storm is getting closer. Through the writhing clouds, black as a father's sin, I see a shape comb together: an outline of limbs, the long loop of a serpentine body.

You could drink lightning out of the air now. I've tried a million times to explain what the monsoon storm smells like: it's two parts petrichor, sure; a little bit of moistened pollution, some variable of rainforest newly baptised in moisture; but mostly, it's this. It's cooked ozone, deep-fried atmosphere, every molecule in the damp air pan-seared in so much electrostatic discharge you could power a small country for days.

"Is there any chance she might have bailed?"

"I mean, it's possible. But I feel like those helicopters are an indication that she hasn't."

"They could just be generic helicopters. There's a chance." I'm still wrapping my brain around the idea that the Internet isn't just sapient, but also a woman named Amanda, while simultaneously *not* a woman named Amanda. Fitz said something about clones. At this point, anything is possible. Particularly doom.

"A really, really small fucking chance."

"Yes. But probably not smaller than our chances of surviving an angry dragon god. I don't know if you were aiming to be reassuring, because if you were, I'm going to have to point out that you're really bad at the whole 'comforting someone worried about imminent death by dragon' thing. Just saying."

Like any other subordinate of the hells, I've died a few times. Knife wounds, explosions, minotaur-related disagreements, voluntary and incredibly athletic decisions to stop my own heart. The usual. But I've never been chewed up and digested by a dragon god. Which, I guess, is a class of experience above being eaten by a garden-variety lizard.

Nonetheless, despite the empirical prestige of a death of this magnitude, I've never felt the urge to add such an event to my glossary of bad endings, a list that is already profanely and profoundly long. "On the off chance that Amanda isn't going to come through, can we please, you know, *go?*"

"Okay, now it's my turn to be real with you. I have

no reason to yank your chain. As far as I'm concerned, we're two peas in the same banged-up pod. I'm a Chronicler and you're... something that prophecy, or premonition, or whatever the fuck this is, has declared to be relevant to the salvation of the universe—"

"Does it come with benefits?"

"What?" You can almost hear the needle of the record player jump and scratch in his mind.

"Being one of the, uh, chosen ones. Does it come with benefits?"

Fitz pauses. "You mean like... dental?"

"Yeah. Or, you know, like, whatever the divine equivalent of an EPF—"

"The fuck is an EPF?"

"Something like a 401k? I don't know. Government-mandated pension or something. My life choices haven't really left me in a position to understand how all that works—"

"I—" He pinches the bridge of his nose and then, as an apparent afterthought, carefully slurps up a measure of his teh tarik. "Is this how I sound to other people? I've been told I do the snarky urban hero thing, but—"

"Do you do run-on sentences? Babble in the face of danger? Wisecrack at encroaching death?" I count sins along my knuckles. In all transparency, I've not always been accepting of the fact I might be an archetype, a tried-and-true neo-anti-hero or whatever it is that pundits call pawns of the cosmic narrative. Not until that one week when a prophecy went a bit awry and Chinatowns across North America grew heaped with dead protagonists, every last one of them victim to the Goldilock phenomenon. Prophecy doesn't like it when their character ensembles aren't quite right. Too short, too blonde, too educated, too predisposed to the wrong kind of quips. Any of these flaws can be cause for omission.

And by 'omission,' of course, I mean that prophecy murders the ones who don't fit.

Long story short, I spent the week stationed in Processing and by the time I was done, denial had crumbled in the wake of grim fact. There's a certain quality to the demographic that I forced to recognize in myself. That or lobotomize myself to avoid the fact.

Anyway.

"I—maybe?"

"In that case, yeah. Probably. It's a calling. Or a linguistic tic. One or the other." I drop my hands, slot my thumbs in my pockets, look longingly at my indomee goreng congealing on its oily plate. I'd asked for it with chicken, and the mamak took my plea to heart. It wasn't just a cold cross-section of breast meat that they'd given me. No, a man somewhere, sepulchred in smoke, had lovingly shredded that arch of chicken thigh, refried all the relevant bits, lovingly wefted it into my noodles. He had even drizzled the crunchy detritus that comes with all Malaysian fried chicken: breading and curry leaves and spices, clots of perfectly crisped fat.

I really, really wanted to sit down and enjoy that meal.

Forget the preceding entree. I wanted *that* meal.

"Ugh."

"You're telling me." The storm swirls closer, bringing with it Ao Qin, he who is cataclysm manifest, his body now coroneting the summit of Sunway Pyramid, Malaysia's misguided attempt at appropriating ancient Egyptian aesthetics, all in the worship of consumerism. I've often wondered where they were going with this, if the architects had understood the connotations of entombing so many shops in those walls. Not that it matters right now. Not with a dragon, lazily slithering up the spine of the shopping complex's sphinx. Though far away, I can see how Ao Qin's torso is teethed with legs, so many legs, because Chinese dragons are not, despite history's enthused insistence, quadrupedal but are distressingly millipedal instead.

The helicopters pull up beside the dragon god, a halo of metallic bodies, no more intimidating than a cloud of fruit flies.

"If I had any inkling as to what to do asides from

stand here and wait for Amanda to finally give the signal, I'd tell you. But I don't." There. In his face, I discern at last what I was hoping I wouldn't see: shining faith, burning like godhead in his eyes. The first drops of rain slide from the orange-washed sky and weep onto his face, silvering his skin in tear-stain streams. "It's been so fucking long since I've not known what to do. I don't…"

I lean away from Fitz. Spend thirty-eight years in Malaysia, where the walls breathe myth, where the skyscrapers stand strangled by the drowsing jungle, and you too will learn a knack for knowing when reality is listening to hear what you intend next.

"Okay, cool. We'll just stand here and wait to die. No problem at all. Nothing ground-shatteringly worrying about this."

"This is probably why urban fantasy books don't feature buddy dynamics."

"Probably."

And Ao Qin, who'd had eons to optimize his sense of dramatic timing, chooses that exact moment to speak.

"*Rupert.*"

It is a whisper. It has the percussions of a whisper, a hoarseness, a rasp to the disyllabic utterance, like he'd exhaled it into my ear. Yet it fills the world: my name made strange in the lungs of a god. It is everywhere. Before me, behind me, beside me—

"Fitz."

I pause and peer at the prophet, suddenly aware that the stereoscopic effect isn't quite complete, and what I'm really hearing is Ao Qin's voice being softly mimicked from my left.

"*What*?" His voice is his again but despite the defensiveness, Fitz has the good sense to appear abashed. "It's involuntary."

"Rupert." Ao Qin singsongs again, this time with more feeling. "Do you know how long I've waited? How many hours I've spent thinking about youuu? All that time in the fire, all that time I spent buuuurrning. Never once did I stop thinking about what you did."

It doesn't matter that he is still, empirically speaking, about thirty metres away. It doesn't matter that Fitz and I are on our feet, on the brink of sprinting to the illusion of safety. Ao Qin and I might as well be snout-to-nose, and I might as well already be breathing numinous halitosis. He'd cross that distance before I can think of a profanity to bleat. The only thing any of this changes is that for once, it leaves me convinced there's no reason to speak.

"Come on, Amanda."

Without looking over, I raise a thumbs-up at Fitz. You can never go wrong with positive feedback.

"They let me out, Rupert. Did you know that? I

didn't need to escape. I told them what I was going to do to you and Heaven said, 'why not?' Why not, indeed?" Even from here, I can see how his face had healed wrong, where muscles had gnarled into valleys of scar tissue, where the bones had failed to reknit, where his jaw tilts on its axis, agape forever, and the ribbon of his tongue wicks listlessly from the break.

Gods, by nature, are protean. Look at Zeus; he was everything from a nimbus of water molecules, to an ant, to a forgery of some poor woman's husband. Gods cycle through bodies like tai tais through couture houses. To witness one allowing imperfection, to see a deity mangled, can mean only one thing: Somewhere in those long days of torture, Ao Qin forgot himself.

He forgot that he had a face before his mutilation, forgot there was ever a time when it wasn't splintered cartilage and ruined meat, forgot what it was like when he didn't burn, wasn't always burning. Even from here, I can *smell* Ao Qin, the barbeque sweetness of flesh roasted on the bone.

"Hey, Fitz?"

"Yeah?"

"Any chance you got a magic gun in that coat of yours? Like, maybe something that can kill an immortal? You know, that sort of thing?"

"No. I don't think it'd be anything that can kill—"

"I'm not asking for Ao Qin. I'm asking for me."

"Yeah. Sorry. Still got nothing."

"Damn." I keep my eyes on the dragon. He pours down the building, puddling in coils atop the asphalt, a baroque spectacle in the sodium glare of the streetlights, gold and red, New Year colours, beautiful as a bad idea. "Can we start running yet?"

"Amanda said—"

Ao Qin is almost on the ground and he won't stop grinning, an eighth of his body drawn up and curled like an inverse question mark. "Youuuu."

For the first time, he takes notice of my companion. Fitz stops dead, tongue pinned between his teeth. A bead of red blood wells on its tip. Well, good; fucker's had it way too easy, standing on the sidelines, convinced that nothing he does will have any consequence.

"I see you, little prophet. I can feel your needling. I know what you did. But it won't woooork. I will eat you when I'm done with Rupert. And I will keep you alive. I will make sure you stay alive for a *long* time in my belly, little prophet. Yessss—"

It is at that precise moment that the helicopters suddenly dart into motion, a three-dimensional octagon of steel, trapping Ao Qin between them. Before Fitz and I can comment, before Ao Qin can even look up, lightning judders from the firmament and, broken to glints by the helicopter blades, impales Ao Qin with white light.

"Okay," says a female voice. "*Now* you idiots can run."

TWO

"I still don't see why I couldn't grab some clothes first."

"I don't know if you remember, but there was a dragon intent on killing you." Amanda tilts a friendly smile at the teenaged cashier at the fro-yo counter, a bored Malay girl of about nineteen. No doubt she's heard the whole conversation, but airports at 4 a.m. teem with people tripping on anything that'd provide respite from the wait. Two sweaty ang-mohs and a dog-tired Chinese uncle talking about dragons and the end of the world. She's probably seen worse. "You still haven't said 'thank you.'"

"I guess I owe you that much." I dig into my jellybean mountain. I may have skipped the yoghurt, went straight into toppings instead, and my cup might be nothing but colourful, gelatinous sweets. Or it may not. I'll never tell. "Thanks."

Amanda inclines her head. "You're welcome."

At first glance, Amanda is the paragon of normalcy. Brown hair, brown eyes, pleasant features, her build athletic but unremarkable. She could be any other corporate thirtysomething, honed by Pilates and largely healthy eating, her attire emblematic of every office lady at rest: white blouse, pencil skirt, flat shoes, a bright scarf for a pop of colour.

On second glance, that's the problem.

Amanda is a composite image. She's a Google Search's worth of faces melted together, every stock image of 'office secretary' and 'yoga mom' blended into a single discrete whole. A literal everywoman, down to the brown of her hair and the specific beige of her complexion. Which, if you think about it, is the perfect look for the Internet. Amanda cocks an inquiring look in my direction, and I flush. Although it has never been articulated, I get the sense that my head is, at least to her personal perception, entirely porous, and all my private thoughts are as ostentatiously visible as sushi on a conveyor belt.

"So." I leaf through my vocabulary for the right words. "Are you a hologram?"

She laughs, exchanging a look with Fitz, who shrugs and drains his water bottle for the umpteenth time. While I still resent Amanda for not procuring me a goodie basket full of James Bond-worthy attire, I'm slightly mollified by the fact she has also left Fitz in a similar predicament. His sweat has dried into continents of damp salt, crusting the ring of his collar, the underside of his armpits, whole sections of his back. Even his thighs have sodium deposits.

"No. I'm real. Flesh and marrow. But." Her eyes flick to Fitz.

"But she's a clone."

"What?"

"Vat-grown clone, with a downloaded personality," Amanda declares, chirpy as a commercial. "It's a long story."

My eyebrows go up. "We've got time."

"He isn't wrong." Fitz bobs his head at Our Lady of Digital Pornography and makes room on the plastic bench, allowing Amanda to sidle up into our table. "We've got, *fuck*, five hours to kill."

Her face goes rigid halfway through Fitz's estimations, expression turned temporarily mannequin-like, before it again adopts a state of exuberant animation. In no way is Amanda what anyone would label a manic pixie dream girl, but there is nonetheless a kind of spiritedness to her, a vivacity that comes across as meticulously manufactured. I suspect again that it has something to do with the fact she is the Internet and there are specific ideas that the Internet has about how a woman needs to behave. "Four hours and twenty-two minutes, but who's counting?"

"Me. Definitely me," I say, although neither of them are paying attention.

Amanda digs a spoon into her yoghurt, mouth pinching with concentration.

"While Amanda figures out fro-yo, I've got a question for you. How much do you know about the new kids in town?"

"They're not bad." My response is automatic. "The God of Missing People, the God of Being Missing. There was a *cat*. Weird as all hell, but at least there's none of the pretentiousness that I—"

"Okay." Fitz stops me with a raised hand. "You met the shock troops, then. But what about the fuckheads up top? Like—"

"There's only one of them." Amanda interrupts. "There's only one guy on top and it's the Man. Everyone else is his... property. Big Money, the Agent..."

From the way her voice tails off, I can tell what she was about to say next. The humour rolls from her expression, leaving it rictused. Fitz stares at Amanda for a minute and stretches out a hand to pat her knuckles, a gesture she receives with a tense, thin smile. Whatever lives these two have led, it likely hasn't enjoyed much affection. Their motions are a minuet of stop-motion awkwardness, like someone had described sympathy to them but forgot to elaborate on the implementation.

"*Were* his property." Fitz tries on a smile. It doesn't work as well as he thinks he does, but I'm too polite to comment aloud. I eat more coloured gelatin. "From what I can tell, the Agent's still happily an, *heh*, agent of the Man. By and large, though, the cornerstones of the modern world aren't designed to be monopolized by authorit—"

Amanda cuts in then. "He doesn't need the exposition. What Fitz is trying to say is the old guard can take any form they want without worrying about fragging their meat, but I can't. I'm not just the idea of global communications and free information, I *am* the Internet. Every damn petabyte of data."

"And if you corporealise in your entirety, your avatar's brain dissolves."

Amanda aims finger-pistols at me. "You got it. So I have clones that I load up with the essentials and pray that they don't move into an area with poor satellite reception, so I can monitor their interactions. In the future, there might be a more efficient solution, but for now, that's it."

"What happens if you get your clone killed?"

"I use another one."

"Or several." Fitz wags his pink plastic spoon at us. Unbelievably, the Chronicler made the healthiest frozen yoghurt choice between the three of us: plain, with a seasoning of digestive biscuits and sliced almonds.

I say nothing for the pour of a minute. When I speak again, my voice is softer than I planned it to be, and there's an ache to the backbeat that I definitely did not want to be there. Usually, I wait until the third date before exposing my sentimental side, but lately, it's been hard not to wear my heart on a sleeve. Between Minah, what happened to Persephone, that thing with Ananke and all those babushkas, I'm just tired these days. Too much pain, too little hope, not enough time to spread between tragedies.

There are nights when I think about that moment before someone pitches themselves in the way of an oncoming train, or from the ledge of a roof, and how many suicide notes begin with a confession of exhaustion.

"Does it hurt?"

"What?"

"When the clones are killed, does it hurt?"

"I never remember it hurting."

The next few minutes are uncomfortable, steeped in a silence that, if broken, would allow for compassion and closer ties. But all at the expense of cool, of decorum, of forfeiting toxic behavioural patterns. So we do nothing. It's like that old joke: an ex-gangster, a mad prophet, and the Internet walk into a fro-yo kiosk—

"What's up with that ink?"

"Thank fucking god." I blow out gustily and tweak my sleeve back, happy to have the subject changed. Under the fabric, my tattoos are a cartographic delirium: non-euclidean maps, star charts for heavens spoked with madness, blueprints to cities with names that bloody the mouth to worship. Sometimes, I dream of these places. I wake up screaming. "They... were a bad idea."

Fitz lets fly a cackle that reverberates through the airport, its notes cutting through the murmured conversations around us. An ang moh couple, so sunburnt their flesh is peeling in red stripes, glares and mumble something in what I think is French. "That's the story I've heard for most tattoos."

"Anecdotal fact," Amanda interjects. "Historically speaking, tattoos have always possessed great symbolism. They're taken to represent something of vast importance, whether religious or otherwise."

"I keep forgettin' I'm hanging around with the spirit of the World Wide Web." His expression sharpens and he returns to me. "Seriously, though."

"I'm a doorway."

Instantly, the pair freeze.

"To where?"

Hell, I almost say. Except that it isn't remotely true. Even given 'hell' isn't strictly an Abrahamic invention, I would be lying. It isn't hell that opens on my skin like a mouth, but something arguably worse or perhaps, better, if you consider the atrocities visited upon us by these pantheons of feral numina. "The spaces outside of existence. Where the Elder Gods live."

"Like, Isis?"

I twirl a hand encouragingly. "Older."

"Inana?"

"No. Older."

"Christ on a heathen trampoline. Fine. I'll let Miss Wikipedia take point."

"Happy to be of service, *asshole*. It must be Dyēus. There are a number of conflicting records, but he is believed to be a chief deity in prehistoric—"

"Older." I pause. "Also more fictional than that. And popular. Board game popular. Parody, YouTube satire, RPG-game-on-Steam popular."

"What?"

"What's Steam?"

Epiphany flashes incandescent in Amanda's eyes. "Oh, fuck me. You're talking about Cthulhu."

"Back up. That squid-head is *real?*" Fitz arrows a look at his yoghurt cup, lifts it up to inspect the underside of the container, a single white drop pearling on the lip as he tilts it. "They put acid in this?"

"The Lovecraftian mythos is beloved by pop culture. Since its conception, numerous people have made the mistake of believing that certain articles belonging to the canon are real. The *Necronomicon*, for example. And as we know, what humanity believes becomes true." The light blinks out of Amanda's face, dims to ash. She squeezes her yoghurt cup until it crumples, spilling white goo over her hands. She doesn't seem to care: her expression is abstracted, eyes full of loss, palms curved and turned up to the light like a penitent in search of a blessing. "But it should take longer than that. More than that."

I glance at the girl in the fro-yo station, unused to this much open discussion, unused to airports in general: she's slouched against the machine, thumbing boredly at her phone. Too familiar, maybe, with the scrutiny of men who should know better, she looks up and bobs eyebrows at me, expression pointed. *What?* It demands. I look away, embarrassed. "Is this a new—?"

"No." Amanda presses her mouth to a line. "Sadly. This isn't… a new development. I've been monitoring the situation. The problem is embryonic, but it is present—"

"I'm concerned about your use of the word 'problem.'" Fitz says.

"I'm concerned about your use of the word 'embryonic.'" I knuckle at my eyes, suddenly hollowed of adrenaline, and I'm tired like I've never been, tired to the gnawed-down tatters of whatever is keeping me upright and awake and cogent enough to speak instead of bleat. "It makes it sound like—"

"Don't interrupt me." Amanda shoots me a cool look.

"Sorry," Fitz and I mumble in tandem.

"But you're on the right track. There have been… incidents across the world." Her lashes, I realize, are improbably long, adorning eyesockets deeper than bruises. I can't tell the colour of her irises anymore, not if they're gold or brown or hazel; but as I stare, they become datapoints in CRT green, matrices of numbers too small to read, so many of them that they transform her corneal tissues into glowing static. The air twitches and I feel the small hairs on the back of my neck climb. "…pods and nurseries, slick as saliva, eggs in the attic, in the bottom of flooded basements, on the bellies of dogs in Chernobyl, everywhere."

"What are you talking about?" Fitz's voice is cigarette-coarse.

"The things from the chain letters, the cryptids, the false-news messiahs. Creepypasta godlings, taking sustenance from the fact that this world is so afraid." She breathes out. "The divide between *then* and *now* has thinned to a fracture. When the first gods were dreamt up, it was by men afraid of the dark, men who needed something, anything to lord over the fire and the stars and to tell them that the sun would rise tomorrow."

"First, there was nothing, and God looked upon that nothing and he said, 'fear,'" Fitz whispers, and the phrase blues the halogen glare. In that new light, Amanda doesn't look quite real, edges smeared, as though of a child's thumb dragged over a fresh Rembrandt. The sensation of static builds, and my ears engorge with noise. "But they're not our problem, though. Right now, Amanda and I are tryin' to find the father gods—"

"Actually, they are."

"What?" Fitz's expression stumbles and he turns to her, a little nonplussed in that way men are, sometimes, when we come home to a house that's been spooned clean of every reason to call it a home. He rakes fingers through dark, lank hair. "I thought—"

Amanda makes a seesaw motion with her hand.

"Yes, but only technically. We *are* trying to find the father gods. We *are* trying to see if we can control the pantheons by taking hold of their piths. None of these motivations exclude an intention to weaponise them against these new gods if necessary."

"What do you mean 'weaponise' them?" Fitz' face closes on itself and he leans back, an infinitesimal tilting of the spine, his chin jutted at the sky,

"Belief is a resource." Her voice keeps a firm grip on its calm. There is nothing to read in those milk-mild features, lineless save for the rare indentations: a few wrinkles bracketing her mouth, her high forehead, not too many or she'd be merely ragged, depreciated by time. Just enough to be human, approachable, appealingly imperfect. If it weren't for the eyes, that is. Glowing, the effluvia of power bleeding from the corners, dripping radium-green onto her lap. "A power source, if you prefer a more hyperbolic assessment. And much like any power source, coal plant or nuclear reactor, it can be tampered with."

"What happens if you do that?"

Amanda shrugs. "Everything dies, I imagine. And if I am right, it'd also cause a chain reaction—"

Images of Demeter and her daughter, faces haloed by the sun, Persephone still learning how to tie freedom around her name like it was her first pair of shoelaces; the Furies and their impartial kindnesses; Houyi and her beloved wife; Veles in his little restaurant, radiant in service, holy again in his joy, they surface and I push up from my seat so quick the chair clatters over.

"I refuse to be a part of this."

"He's not the only one," says Fitz, fists clenched.

"There are two options." Amanda plows on, inexorable, monstrous in her placidity, her certainty, that look on her face that is halfway between pity and impatience. It would have been better if she'd shouted, if she'd tried hot-wiring my will to her command. Violence is as easy as a broken nose. After the first time, you learn the crunch and the yaw, how to keep your head up, keep ahead of the pain banging like a second heart in the dome of your mouth. "You help me or you don't."

"Seems like a really obvious choice to me," says Fitz. "I choose going home, where I'm not at the risk of being murdered by fucking Jeff the—"

"But he'll kill you, anyway, once he pours into the brains of your species, a species so terrified of its own end that it'd do anything to ignore the fact it is coming. He is going to get into the politicians, the ministers, the pastors, the popes, the people who shape your stupid simian society. And at some point, one of them is going to go 'why not?' when he gives them a little nudge, and that will set off a chain reaction—"

"*Stop.*"

"—and it will all come falling down like dominos, and people will kill in the name of whatever polled better on social media, and there will be nothing you can do because all this new pantheon wants is for you to self-destruct, singing praises of the shotgun shell."

I crack my jaw to object again, louder this time, because Guan Yin knows the first attempt didn't work. Then the universe ripples. Think of creation as a kuih lapis, or an onion, or the stratums of skin, each of which contains entire macrocosms of blasphemies and miracles. Our reality sits shivering at the pith with its hands over its eyes, but there is always something happening in the adjacent layers and if you know how to look the right way, tilt your head so the light bends into myth, you can see straight through them.

And sometimes, you can see the things on the other side looking right back.

"Fuck." I swallow around a lungful of sudden terror.

"That's the thing about gods," Amanda continues, softly, not making eye contact with either of us, an entire cosmology of unborn deities curled embryonic in the air around her, waiting, nascent, nacreous, a caul of verdigris over faces that are still suggestions. And from each of them extends umbilical cords that spindle around the axis of Amanda's spine. There has always been a mother goddess in every culture. Makes sense that the Internet is ours. "Humanity likes to pretend that gods are above them, calved from animal desires. But the truth is that they're not, we're nothing but the apparatus your species uses to examine its fears."

She breathes out and in the hinge between seconds, something abandons Amanda, the enormity of presence that scaffolded her person. She shrinks. She becomes human, husked of that indifferent glory, so much *ache* threaded through her expression that I can't hold her tired eyes with mine.

"If you're not going to help me save the world," she says, "you can at least help me save *me*."

"Goddamnit," Fitz pushes a finger up the bridge of his nose. "How the fuck do you expect anyone to say 'no' to something like that?"

THREE

"Passport?"

I study the man sitting straight-backed at the counter, glaring at me through the bullet-proof glass separating us, his bald head bulbous with veins. There's something distinctively martial about both his appearance and the aggression bunched behind his expression, the machinery of his vocation barely adequate to contain the latter. I get the feeling he'd leap over the barrier to strangle me if he could. I don't blame him; given the circumstances, I'd throttle me too.

"You saying what ah? I got passport? Got." The Malaysian accent is not one of those easily categorisable as 'attractive,' not least because it is distinctively Asian in timbre, a regional lilt which only ever fills the West with laughter. Frequently, it is associated with stupidity, a lack of education, although I've always had trouble understanding that. Incompetent bilingualism is sexy in any accent, but you're an idiot if you speak perfect English like a Chinaman. Still, there's value in prejudice: people rarely think to keep their guards up around those they see as their lessers. "Got passport."

He glares.

"Give me your passport." He spits each word in staccato succession, anger simmering in the delivery.

"Got give already at last airport."

The trouble with a sudden exodus from your country precipitated by the assault of a dragon, the advent of a prophecy, and the promise to save a goddess from an unwanted litter of nightmares, is that these things seldom include practicalities like luggage, appropriate wardrobes, and a stop home to pick up your passport. In fairness, Amanda had been more than excellent at defanging some of those issues, but the Malaysian immigrant is much easier to cow than the vanguard of American paranoia.

Also, she's at least seven families behind me in the

queue and there's no way the TSA will allow her and Fitz to fumble to the front.

"Fucking..." he swears under his breath. His eyes flit to my wrists, where my sleeves had ridden up, revealing my tattoos, the banged-up knuckles, and the scars torquing down along the bones of my hand, at least three quarters of which were inflicted by drunk cooking. "That isn't how the system works. If you want to come into the country, you show me your passport. So, give me your fucking passport."

I ransack my pockets, making a show of it. "Have to give you meh?"

"Yes."

"You sure ah?"

Still no telltale commotion behind me, no indication that Amanda and Fitz might have liberated themselves from courtesy to save me from being incarcerated. My pockets reveal nothing but lint, a few dust bunnies lolling around in the dark. This won't end well. I suppose, if I wanted to review my predicament in a positive light, I at least get to go home.

But if I have one vice, it is commitment to making the world a more decent place for other people.

"Pass. Port." You know an official representative of the state is pissed when they can separate a word into a paragraph, the gap between two syllables as ponderous as a police record.

"Shit." I straighten.

Gong Tau, in my opinion, suffers an unnecessarily atrocious reputation, as do many genuses of so-called black magic. But despite my personal biases, I don't blame people for their suspicion. Holy miracles, for example, rarely demand more than the presence of a neat wooden cross and a splash of consecrated water. The dark arts, by contrast, are invariably messy.

Before the TSA employee—Bob, a bronze badge on his broad chest declares—can demand my documentation again, I gash my thumb open with my teeth. Blood slops onto the counter, causing Bob to recoil out of his seat, his stool toppling over. I think I can hear Amanda, shouting over the panic flexing through the crowd. I can definitely hear airport security.

But they're not here yet, which is the part that matters.

I slap the glass with my bloodied palm and utter, at a machine-gun cadence, the words of a spell, an invitation, a summoning. Nothing especially formal, but the advantages of 'evil'—and do note the quotation marks there—magic is that it operates on nuance, not inviolate scripture. The demon that peels itself from my shadow, shucking the dark like a layer of unwanted skin, is unsettlingly tall, utterly bereft of hair, and possesses a head that is nothing but a prism of rotting infant faces.

"Hey."

It narrows its myriad eyes. "Hi."

"So, you remember that card game we had?"

"Yeah?"

"The one where I said you could defer your payment, because you were broke, and it was seven weeks to the Hungry Ghost Festival, and there was no way in, haha, hell that you could pay me back right then?"

"No."

"I'm calling that favour in." Time is deterministic. It banks on an arbour of rules, mechanisms that many have likened to clockwork, with interlocking parts and a certain bull-headed intransigence when it comes to barrelling from point A to point B. But that is the mortal perspective. In the presence of the supernatural, time becomes iffy.

Or more accurately, rather like taffy.

"I said no."

I stare at the encroaching security detail, the world a wash of amber. "Please?"

"No."

"Look at how nicely I'm asking."

Exasperation colours the demon's faces puce. "No."

"I'm going to point out that you technically have no choice here, because of the whole rules-of-engagement thing, but I am absolutely willing to throw in an extra packet of Gudang Garam, if you'd just do this for me." Even magic cannot stop the law, only impede its approach. For an airport, Orlando possesses some phenomenally well-built muscle, hulking quarterbacks that could easily audition for the role of God's Wrath in a Broadway take on the Old Testament. "Please?"

Cigarettes are currency. Take it from me. In prison, in the Ten Hells, in any environment where people of dubious morals are coerced into cohabitation. I don't know *why* specifically; my vices, as a rule, are more epicurean in nature. But cigarettes, ang moh. If you're ever in doubt, put a crumpled pack of smokes on the table, and chances are you'll be in a better position than you were before.

At the very least, what follows will probably hurt infinitesimally less.

"Fine."

He steps into me, a single loose-jointed motion. I ricochet out of my body, feeling, for an instant, bone and brain deform, warping around a will separate from mine.

To explain: the process of duplicating a human isn't easy. Hollywood makes it stylish, but like everything else, it's not so much a flourish as a science brined in effluvia. To make a human, you must first *understand* the human, a process that simultaneously involves deciphering the atoms of the unfortunate simian and a visual effect that, I am told, resembles making cotton candy out of meat floss. As with everything infernal in origin, it's an unpleasant process, both for the perpetrator and the victim. It's why demons mostly take possession. It's a lot less work.

But then it is over.

I stagger upright, wiping the back of my hand over my mouth. I am three feet away from where I had previously stood, standing in a tenebrous slope of shadow and solidly on American soil. Behind me, grinning at Bob, both palms bleeding and pressed to the glass, is the demon borrowing my face, a perfect replica, down to the dwindling cover on his pate. You know what they say: nothing is certain save for death, taxes, and male pattern baldness.

Time accelerates. The burly guards rubberband forward, leaping through the air, and hit my doppelganger together. It is a comedic moment. I'm not a big man: five-eight, when I care enough to not slouch; rounder than I was when I cracked skulls for the Triads, closer in appearance to a well-compensated chef than a criminally underpaid thug, but still disproportionately lanky. The security detail, conversely, are not those things.

The demon flails my arms. By and large, it is the only part of him that you can see under a homoerotic snarl of spectacularly ripped bodies. I move away before anyone thinks to look in my direction. Optimistically, this is where they book him and discover, hours after the fact, a slurry of meat in wherever they'd chosen to detain him and decide, to a man, that no one is ever to speak of this moment again.

When in doubt, use demons.

"WHAT THE FUCK, Rupert?"

"Come on, they were going to take me in."

"What the ever loving fuck?" Amanda repeats. The exit to Orlando International Airport is teeming with excited children and their exasperated parents, a few surly teenagers, and couples who, for some reason, believe that Disneyland is a better honeymoon destination than the genteel balconies of Paris or— anywhere not otherwise swarmed by sugar-drunk kids. "It was a bloodbath. If you'd just fucking gone quietly and asked for a lawyer, this could have been done more discreetly."

"I'm allergic to lawyers." I shrug out of my hoodie. Florida isn't what I was expecting. I blame popular culture. America, in my brain, is either red desert, prairie the colour of skin and the smell of sun-bleached bone, or something green and dark and cold, fizzing grandly on the tongue. I'd expected anything but the unctuous heat of Malaysia, sticky, sauna-like, suspiciously similar to being smothered to death by a warm towel. And I think I want a refund. "Even the thought of them gives me the creeps."

"For fuck's sake." Amanda rolls her eyes so hard I hear it in her voice. We're waiting for what is allegedly another clone of Amanda's to come pick us up, so we may adjourn to the ritzy Best Western that she had booked us into. Despite the fact that Amanda could, in both practice and theory, home us in the grandest of Hiltons, she won't, pleading the need for anonymity. I suspect she doesn't like us as much as she claims.

"In fairness," says Fitz, taking a drag from his third cigarette of the hour, "it was funny."

"Thank you! Someone who appreciates my art!"

"Art." Amanda grinds out an incredulous laugh. "And I thought Reddit had terrible opinions."

I shade my eyes against the noon-day glare and frown. The sky is gorgeous, a faultless blue groping towards forever. Despite my best efforts at being a curmudgeon, it's hard not to become infected with the excitement buzzing through the crowd, anticipation a more efficient disease than even the common cold, regardless if the vector might be oversized mouse ears. I flick a glance back at Fitz and Amanda, the two of them now engrossed in an argument about hot breakfasts and the legitimacy of British bacon. My scowl deepens.

It takes me a minute, but I realize why I'm rankling against the experience. This is pleasant. All of it. Forget the fact I've just drenched immigration in bodily fluids and dispatched a demon into their custody, albeit one who most likely won't do anything but lightly traumatise the airport personnel. This moment feels companionable, comfortable.

And I don't trust it at all. Good things happen to the morally ambiguous hero, not the guy who makes amuse-bouches of ears.

A black SUV screeches up to the pavement before I have the opportunity to further interrogate my paranoia. The window winds down. Inside, there's a woman who could well have been Amanda's aunt: same jawline, same incline to the cheekbones. Her eyes are obscured by aviator glasses, and where Amanda keeps her hair in a neat ponytail, this one wears hers in a bouffant worthy of any Hong Kong tai tai.

"Get in the van."

I look between the two of them. "Whoah."

"Yeah, in case you're wondering, that never stops getting weird." Fitz twitches a shoulder at me, slinking past as the two Amandas mouth curses at his back, the one-point-five second lag between them causing no small amount of aural dissonance. I've sometimes wondered what it would be like to survive the technological singularity. I don't wonder anymore and I deeply regret the fact.

"Great," I mumble, following Fitz into the mouth of suburban weird.

THERE'S A *LARGENESS* to Orlando that I don't think I was prepared for. Malaysia, small enough, from one end of the peninsula to the other, to traverse in a day, is a knot of cramped streets and labyrinthian highways, overgrown with plant life. London, in its own fashion, wasn't much different. You can tell it was built for horses.

But America.

Film cannot convey the immensity of the country, how it balloons in your consciousness, fills you with the dizzy ambition of it all. America is earnest. For all of its problems, its clandestine bigotry, its history and its horrors, it is earnest as a dog with a jaw full of dead squirrel. You can practically feel it tail-wagging through the asphalt.

Also, there are an odd number of palm trees here.

"Does this mean we're not going to Disneyland?" Fitz lounges across the back seat like a cat, one leg hooked companionably over mine. "Because that will be disappointing."

"I feel like you're just fucking with me now." The

Amandas, one riding shotgun, the other steering one-handed, an arm crooked out of a window, have given up on talking in tandem. Instead, their mouths now move noiselessly, while a voice crackles from the radio. The effect is still unfathomably disconcerting, but at least it is easier to stomach, so long as I keep my eyes somewhere else.

"Maybe," says Fitz. "I mean, you're kinda fun to annoy. It's one thing to outwit the gods, but it's another thing to piss off the spirit of pure knowledge."

"Again, not a spirit."

"That's a reference, isn't it?" I rummage through the duffle bag that Amanda Sr had bestowed on us. There are gaudy Hawaiian shirts in citrus colors, most of them too big, one of them likely intended for an infant, khaki shorts to be paired with flip-flops, boxers, bedazzled Ray-bans, and a heap of gold chains. "The hell?"

I raise the jewellery for inspection, but neither Amanda looks over, although I'm sure the corner of Amanda Jr's mouth crimped fractionally in amusement. "It seemed appropriate."

"A decent suit would have been appropriate too. Haven't you watched gangster movies?" I sift through the mess again, hoping half-heartedly that somewhere in the bag I'd find, if not grayscale, then at least less offensively cheerful attire. "Lots of rumpled jackets and silk ties."

"This is Florida, though," Amanda retorts gaily. "You'll fit in better this way."

I don't reply. I toss Fitz a selection of shirts: red, blue, and white alligators against a luridly tropical backdrop of green-gold palms and ambiguously ethnic-looking women, as some might put it, what with the racist shorthands used by the artist. To my relief, he swaps his filthy wife-beater for the first of the set, flinging the discarded garment out of a window and into the way of a Corvette. The driver narrowly dodges the fluttering horror, swears up a hurricane at us, flicks Fitz the finger, and peels off to the right.

For myself, I finally find a hospital-beige shirt with pineapples. As much as I would like to shuck my jeans along with the grubby pair of boxers sticking to their insides, I can't bring myself to do so. It would be an admission of middle age—or worse, that the ang mohs who flounce around Kuala Lumpur might actually be right about less-is-more in the equatorial sauna.

"Huh."

"What?" Fitz, unlike yours truly, has no cultural misgivings about shorts or exposing hirsute testicles to the freeway. Or me. Ugh.

"Cason's already there, it looks like."

"Who's Cason?" I'm not sure who says it, Fitz or I, but it doesn't matter. Exposition must take place.

Except it doesn't.

"He has done reconnaissance at the university already. Says that no threats were registered." Back to that unwieldy practice of massaging air through the larynx, I suppose, although this time, Amanda's decided it would be better to distribute responsibility of the sentence between two mouths, the pair of them start-stopping in creepy twin fashion. Oddly, that's still more reassuring than the lag.

"Who's Cason?"

We zip past a billboard that entreats us to *come have a hoedown* with a heaving meat-mountain of a burger. I count four patties between the dribbles of cheese.

"I don't know if I trust his opinion. Cason's on a different level, you know what I'm saying?" Fitz, with supernatural deftness, begins rolling a fresh cigarette. "The fucking apocalypse could come and all he'd have to say on the topic is, 'there was an inconvenience.'"

"He's not stupid."

"Seriously, who's Cason?"

"Then why did he spend so many fucking years stuck blowing coke up Eros's ass? Has it occurred to you that he might have an agenda of his own?" Fitz exhales, and the smell of weed plumes through the air. "That he might be looking for some way to buy back all the things he's lost?"

"If he was, he wouldn't be the Lamp."

I roll my eyes to the ceiling, the navy faux-velvet

pockmarked with stains. "Oh, great. More things I don't know."

"He could be the Lamp and an asshole." Fitz jerks a thumb at me. "Case in point."

"I prefer *wiseass*, personally."

"Even so," says Amanda Senior, chin dipping, even as Amanda Junior raises her jaw. "That doesn't change the fact that they're part of this. You're the one who told me this."

"Someone? Anyone? I know you're just ignoring me."

"The Lamp, the Road, the Door and the Knife," Fitz recites, voice strange and rolling, that electric hum twitching through the air again, and suddenly, the inside of the SUV is cottony with a taste of static. "After our pow-wow with the old gods—"

"Where Fitz basically threatened the entirety of creation."

"We really need to circle back to that, at some point." I dot the air with a finger, as though to bookmark the moment.

"—I had a vision. Which could well have been just a hallucination."

"For the last time, morels are not that kind of mushroom."

"You two have a problem communicating information clearly and effectively."

"The father gods on a land of glass, their faces turned to an ocean black," Fitz whispers, and now, now he has the rhythm of prophecy to his voice, that roiling timbre, half-here in reality, half elsewhere, his soul moulded into a mouthpiece. "They see a way out. Down through the belly of earth, down where even the gods won't go. But there is a road that will take the willing to them and at the end, there is a door and a knife. The Lamp will show us the beginning. The Knife will see us to an end."

"What end? Also, who the *fuck* is Cason?"

They look over, all three of them, an act that has us swerving alarmingly into a copse of palm trees. I scream. Fitz turns, joins in a high-octave warbling chorus. The Amandas, unsurprisingly, only glance sidelong at the encroaching catastrophe. At the last moment, we turn away, the SUV scraping along the body of a tree. The screech almost drowns out what follows.

"Cason's the half-human son of the Devil." Fitz does one of his shrugs, suddenly the icon of insouciance yet again. "That's all."

"Oh. Is that it? Is that all? Well, in *that* case—"

"—SERIOUSLY, WHY DIDN'T you think it would be a good idea to tell me these things?"

Amanda Jr—who is now again the solitary Amanda, her counterpart having driven off, tear ducts drooling blood—cants a look at me. "We figured it wasn't that important."

"It is important to know when you're going into business with people dealing with the Devil."

"You work for Hell."

"Diyu, thank you." I pause. "And that's different."

She plants a fist along the indent of a narrow hip, eyebrows raised to the roof of the world. The day persists in being uncomfortably attractive, the blue a colour from the palette of god. Saturated in sunlight falling slantwise over its roofs, our Best Western looks veritably palatial. "How is it different?"

"Diyu is a place of rehabilitation. Abrahamic Hell is just barbaric."

"Uh huh."

"The idea behind the Eighteen Levels of Chinese Hell is that at the end of your sentence, you'll emerge a better entity, purified, ready to again enter the cycle of reincarnation—"

"You have a hell that involves putting sinners in a *steamer.*"

"The Chinese culture is intimately tied with food."

"I guess that explains the pan-frying in oil as well." Fitz adjusts the positioning of the duffle bag, easing it up and over his collarbone with a shrug. Amanda

Senior, who is allegedly all right, who is certainly *not* endeavouring to career down the side of a cliff, removing proof of our existence and freeing up resources for use by the distributed consciousness of the World Wide Web, wasn't much of a fashion maven, but she knew the value of gold. Which makes me miss her, but the Internet doesn't care about individuals. Least of all those it grows on a carbon-fibre umbilical cord in an undisclosed location.

"And that hell where you're force-fed lava."

"*Really* enlightened," Fitz drawls, a shit-eating grin spreading across the whole of his face. "I gotta ask. What does it smell like down there?"

Like my every day, I almost say, but I curb stomp the compulsion. It's too soon. I suspect it will not stop feeling like it is too soon, not while I can still smell German tourists crisping in the oven, that fatty tenderness I've come to associate with human meat because texturally speaking, we're not too different from low-grade wagyu. You would think that Hell reeks of the abattoir, but truth is that it smells like the kitchen of a king.

"Like bad decisions," I manage, and if either of them notice the hitch in my voice, they give no comment. Fitz winks at a coy, luminous, young, brown-haired thing as she saunters past, earning giggles and air kisses, all in spite of the fact Fitz resembles a pimp from the set of Miami Vice.

Amanda holds my eyes for longer than I'd have liked, longer than I can still my breath, and I'm about to tell her *don't make it weird* when she lets loose a fluting laugh. "Touché."

I swallow. I wonder how much they know.

We file into the reception area, which is sterile and spacious, liberally doused with whatever it is that the international cabal of hotels had long ago unanimously agreed would be their signature scent. I swear on Guan Yin's painted toenails, there's no other explanation. It's the same smell everywhere, even when the wallpapers are soaked through with gore: a frantic, pine-infused cheer. Similarly, the receptionist who greets us could be any of the hotel employees I've ever encountered: enamelled hair, gleaming smile, a kind of predatory alertness, bringing to mind a Shiba Inu in sight of a small, soon-to-be-dead squirrel.

"Ma'am."

He runs his gaze over us. I'd expected the practiced amiability to falter, compromised by the fact we're two idiots in beachwear and a woman of ambiguous ethnicity, a duffel bag between us and nothing else. We have to look like fugitives or a polyamorous triad intent on a brisk, athletic kink.

"Amanda Doe. We're looking to check in."

"*Really.*"

She ignores me. "It's been a long flight and we lost our baggage."

The receptionist swaps his expressions, trading 'impersonal friendliness' for 'curated concern,' the change so abrupt that it makes me recoil. He fixes each of us with thirty seconds' eye contact, head bobbing, before he concludes the gesture with a smooth, "Sorry to hear that. We'll send you a bottle of wine. It's the least we can offer."

Amanda nods, slapping a credit card atop the countertop, her movements as rehearsed as his. The smile, too, a tiny upturning of her mouth to complement the way the light oils across her hair. It is all frankly unsettling, what with the cognitive dissonance that comes from knowing that Amanda, for all her secretarial elegance, is a goddess hoping to abort her demon children before they can infect reality.

Speaking of which, no one's discussed this fact anywhere near enough.

I jot down a mental note to remedy this, while the receptionist busies himself with procuring us access to our temporary habitats. Three keycards, specifically. To *two* rooms. I suspect the wine will route itself to Amanda's personal sanctuary, but hope rules eternal.

"Fitz and I are taking the suite. You get the weird double." Amanda passes me my keycard, an apologetic shrug in accompaniment.

Better than nothing. "Beats having to share a room with either of you."

"Hah." Fitz glances back at the receptionist, the man's smile still gelled in place. "Looking forward to alone time with Cason?"

"I was assuming he had his own accommodations?" I glare, letting my voice rise on the last syllable, a question in its tail.

"He does." Amanda has taken to scanning the environment slowly, skull travelling too far in one direction and then the other, enough to make me wince. No wonder she churns through clones so quickly. "Cason doesn't like sharing his personal space when he doesn't have to."

I bite my tongue hard enough to choke on the pain. Too easy to think that a life with Eros is all orgiastic fun and an all-you-can-fuck buffet of naked bodies. As a species, as a man, you're flat-out conditioned to make that joke. But it doesn't require much to put two and two together, and figure, with waxing horror, how bad that can be when you want nothing of what might be involved. Small wonder Cason prefers to be left alone.

"He'll"—green twitches, neon and wild, across Amanda's brown eyes—"convene with us after he's had something to eat. In the meantime, get some rest. We'll do the same."

Fitz taps two fingers to the side of his forehead, his eyes bruised purple with exhaustion. Neither of us had really slept during the long flight to Florida, but I wonder when Fitz had eight hours to call his own. His sallow complexion and the microscopic facial tics are clues to an unpleasant truth. Wisecracking is symptomatic of trauma; at least, in my personal experience. I study Fitz, silent, as we enter one of the lime-scented elevators, a child and her blonde mother taking the opposite corner.

The pair exit on the third floor, although not before Fitz conjures a pair of clean boxers to toss at me, blowing a kiss and an entreaty to call him. The mother, for all the haute implied by her hundred-dollar bangs, only muffles her sniggering, while her daughter stares, wide-eyed and uncomprehending.

"Tell you when you're older," I mumble, wadding up the underwear and cramming it into a pocket, too tired to be embarrassed.

A droll mechanical voice announces that we've arrived on the seventh floor. I stagger out. I want a shower. I want to lie on clean sheets. I want sleep. Mostly, I want a world where I wake up to nine-to-five doldrums, to a wardrobe full of pastel shirts, a job that requires only the punch-card worship of daily attendance, a wife who tolerates me, mediocre children, a dog, *maybe*, of suspicious pedigree and reasonable intelligence, and tedium, nothing but sweet tedium. I want a life so *staggeringly* boring that I dream nightly of a dragon god, burning up inside, roasting on the spit of his own spine.

But I'll take a shower first.

And maybe, a haircut.

"THE WHOLE 'SAVING the world' business isn't that bad, right?"

Fitz crosses his arms behind him and leans back, xylophone chest on display.

He has a point. This *is* nice. A faint crusting of algae floats along the margins of the pool, sure, but the declining sun flatters everything, including errant eukaryotic colonies. I might even say that the dusk has rendered them gorgeous.

"Maybe," I concede, relaxing onto my lounge chair. Much to Amanda's chagrin, Cason still hasn't made an appearance. Apparently, somewhere in Orlando, an excellent rodízio churrascaria is regretting its policy on how many times you can request more slabs of meat. An extraction is currently taking place, leaving Fitz and I to do nothing but bask in the warmth. "Just maybe."

"If it helps," Fitz looks over the rim of his sunglasses, smirking. "Amanda says we're free to order room service."

"But does American room service deliver, er, outside rooms?"

"Who the hell knows? Doesn't hurt to ask. We're in Florida. The weather's great. We're probably going to die horribly sometime next week. But for now, we're here, we're alive, we have unlimited money to spend in a shitty Best Western. Take advantage of it."

"I guess you're right." Against my will, the tension loosens from my shoulders. Fatalistic as his proclamation might be, Fitz has a point again. Tomorrow, we perish; today, we exist in the lap of moderate-to-adequate luxury. "So, you think the fish here's going to be any good. I could murder for a—"

And it is right then, of course, that an alligator decides to fucking eat me.

FOUR

Take it from me.

It is hard to breathe through a punctured lung; particularly, and I would like to strongly emphasise this for the benefit of future generations, when the object responsible for said perforation is still embedded in the chest cavity. I gargle blood as the world blurs into a blue-green blaze, unable to decide how I'm going to die: asphyxiating on my own fluids, eaten by the reptile that has absconded with me, or having my skull cracked against the pavement as my body flip-flops in its jaws.

My legs are definitely broken.

If I still had anything resembling a voice, or a larynx that isn't stoppered with bile, I might scream, but right now, it is difficult to do anything but expire at a rate appropriate to the situation.

('Quickly,' in case that wasn't obvious already.)

But let's backtrack. Indulge, maybe, in the fact that history is penned by the survivors and creative license is par for the course. Though I cannot be sure, what with the fact my head is bouncing along the asphalt and my viewpoint of the world currently inverted, I suspect the situation looks rather comical.

Picture: a five-eight Chinese man, in the grip of an alligator, feet dragging along as the reptile barrels towards the underbrush, limp as a doll. He must be colossal. The reptile, not the man. The position in which the alligator has me trapped would no doubt present logistical complications to a smaller specimen: I have an arm prospecting down his gullet, a shoulder pinioned, and judging from the pain clenching my left hip, my kidney's been compromised.

It is getting harder to breathe.

It is getting impossible to breathe.

In different circumstances, I would have allowed nature to take its course. Mastication is unpleasant, but nothing that cannot be recovered from. I've died from bullets, knives, machetes, bicycle whips, every manner of bludgeon, a few exotic poisons, strangulation, immolation, impalement, disembowelment and, once, of spontaneous organ failure. Every single time, I've returned after a short jaunt through Diyu and continued with life as I knew it.

Unfortunately, resurrection isn't without its drawbacks.

As the perspicacious might have guessed already, my reanimation inevitably involves restoring my pre-existing body, my one vessel. It is messy, and frequently redolent of the liquids that a corpse discharges, but it works. This will, naturally, be a problem if I allow the alligator to finish what it has begun. More likely than not, it intends to stash me at the bottom of a river, where I will then drown, rot and puff up accommodatingly, allowing the bastard to disembowel me at relative leisure.

As I say, death or disembowelment is not the part that worries me. What gives cause for significant consternation is the fact that I might be firmly lodged in the bowels of a swamp, unable to escape, unable to do anything but provide ample protein to the local ecosystem, even as I drown in the churning murk over and over again.

So, let's see how we can avoid that.

The asphalt melts into thorny viridian brush. My options are thinning as quickly as the daylight. It's now, or an eternity steeping in the mud.

My mouth is full of salt and spittle, and I have to spit blood as I wrench myself upwards, anchoring my fingers in the reptile's great nostrils. In retaliation, it tosses its head and multiple *somethings* shatter in succession. Fucking *ow*. Muscular control winks out below where my rib cage flares widest and the next time I breathe in, a wet throatful of rust, I feel the splintered end of a bone skewering what I assume to be some sort of organ. Pain glows through my core.

"Motherfucker," I burble, jerking a shoulder upwards. The meat there, between the end of a clavicle and the length of my pectoral, feathers open like a rump roast on its way to becoming to pulled pork: muscle doesn't like being forced to move around a giant tooth. But it gets me what I want, which is the opportunity to free up the other arm, breaking two fingers on its triumphant exit from the alligator's mouth.

Okay, that last part I could have done without, but dinners can't be choosers.

The leviathan rolls a yellow eye in my direction, blinking, and what I don't expect is its shambolic attention, the languorousness of it, as though of a creature sedated and coerced into witnessing its own vivisection. Something is wrong. Apart from everything else, alligators aren't meant to be horned, or feathered, or bewigged in the fashion of the ancient Egyptians, a solar crown rising precariously from the sable mass.

Also, this isn't an alligator. It's a crocodile.

Also—

"I don't know if you realize"—teeth jangle in my mouth; I let my mouth loll open, let them tumble onto the pavement in a clatter of ruined enamel—"but there's something growing out of your head."

True enough, Sobek, Lord of Crocodiles, Pointed of Teeth, He Who Eats While He Mates, and all those epithets Wikipedia insists are associated with this icon of aggressive fecundity, has something blooming from his flat skull, a misshapen tumour largely comprising grey-blue ganglia and oily black hair. At first glance, I almost mistake the growth for a diasporic penanggalan, but then it swivels on the stub of bloody cartilage and fixes me with a grin.

Nope. No penanggalan here, no genteel intellect with a face to shame Aphrodite, the dangling effluvia beautifully flush, gorgeous and radiant as a bouquet of roses. This thing has a lunatic grin and waxen skin, a lidless stare with sockets too big for those bloodshot eyes rolling within. It chatters at me, nonsense noises, and Sobek spasms, slowing. I'm close enough to see the membrane of his great eye twitch, engorging first with black tendrils, before it erupts into gore, worm-like filaments needling through the mess.

"The fuck? Oh, fuck. Oh, fuck. Oh—"

I hyperventilate through obscenities while Sobek roars, thrashing as the thing, the parasite, the tumour, the whatever-the-fuck-it-is burrows deeper into his brain. Unfortunately, he has still yet to let go, although that is no active fault of the crocodilian divinity. I remain brochetted on his dentition. Something unravels from the pit of my stomach and a weight falls loose in loops.

Great. Just great. My intestines snarl like Christmas lights around everything from the shrubbery to Sobek's foot, and the world lurches as something catches and something *tears*. Fuck. It is astonishing what you can survive when you've been rudely inoculated against shock. The lizard brain insists on survival.

Speaking of which, Sobek tosses his mighty head a few more times before at last capitulating to animal instinct. He flings himself down, writhing across the ground, *twisting*—driven, perhaps, by some vague molecule of ancestral memory, a certainty inherited from the dinosaurs: if you pulverize something, it *will* stop biting. But unfortunately, caveats apply.

If the offending organism has already colonised your brain, such methods are likely to prove impotent. Whatever that thing is, it doesn't seem to care, content to continue domesticating the wrinkles of Sobek's cerebral cortex.

Me, on the other hand? *I* care like anything.

I care because it is a one-ton animal *wantonly* applying its weight to the bone-meal remains of my spine. I care because with every circuit, every stomach-turning twist, I am that little bit closer to becoming purée, a smear of questionable colours spread across Orlando. I care because my synapses have begun free-associating, bewildered by this palette of agonies, and I had no idea there were so many bones to snap, so many muscles to rip, intestines ribboning across the air, and I'd scream if I wasn't drowning.

Then something gives.

The turbulence dislodges me from my impalement and I am flung up—up—head over heels over head. The sky is gorgeous, faultless as power, blue and hot. A little delirious, a little chewed-up-by-crocodile, I extend a bloodied hand to the horizon. Gravity elects that moment to reassert itself and the firmament is replaced by the less pleasant sight of the open mouth of a crocodile god.

I vanish headfirst into Sobek's throat, guzzled with less effort than a broken-backed bunny.

All things considered, it could be worse.

* * *

"Ow."

I'm dead. *Finally.*

Relieved, I pat myself down, ecstatic to be whole again. The fact that I am in Diyu is entirely inconsequential. This isn't the first time, and I imagine it won't be the last. Sure, the climate is unexceptional and the less said about the topography the better, but the population trends towards being both courteous and interesting, and I am told they've become infatuated with bubble tea of late. By and large, it could be worse. It could be the stomach of a divine being, each second dilated into a century, your body corroding in the acids, flesh sloughing in foaming tatters.

I unfold to my feet, pushing up from one knee and then another, an inventory of my limbs taken yet again. There is one consolation to the whole situation. Ordinarily, transitioning from the mortal realm to Diyu is an experience like no other, pain of a magnitude that words have failed to concisely encapsulate. But it would appear that my entanglement with Sobek was so profoundly agonizing it supplanted my awareness of the journey.

A pair of shadows wash over me, accompanied by animal musk.

"You shouldn't be here." Ox-Head has a slow, placid voice, the kind you'd expect of a well-fed herbivore.

"There are a few people still angry at you, Rupert." Likewise, Horse-Face's speech is serene, self-assured. His diction says, *This is a stallion of means, confident of his prowess, bereft of any need to assert his dominance, so prodigious his reproductive abilities, so exquisite his genetics. Look upon him and delight in his calm temper, his even gait.*

"You are lucky none of them is Yan Luo."

The trick to dealing with these two is ignoring the structural dissonance of their mandibles, and taking no note of their respective maxilla. It isn't even that their teeth are unsettlingly carnivorous in architecture. It's the way they fit.

"I mean, as long as he isn't pissed at me." I dust myself off. "Are you two pissed at me, by any chance?"

They exchange looks. Both Horse-Face and Ox-Head have always been of variable height, never precisely as tall as you think they are, always worse than you expect. Today, however, they take especial care to loom menacingly. But it doesn't work. After the day I had it feels like home, the posturings of cousins on the first night of Chinese New Year, when everyone is in competition about who has done better for themselves.

Before they can speak, I add: "I missed you guys, by the way. Like, *seriously* missed you guys. I know we've had some rough times, been through a few arguments.

You've even killed me, too. But all in all, I like you guys. I don't think I've ever said that."

They trade looks again, caution tensing in their eyes.

"A trick, Rupert?" Horse-Face purrs, sibilant as he breathes, and all despite that there is none of the right consonants. Ox-Head, scowling, tilts his polearm at me.

I raise my palms with a grin. "No. No, I *swear*. Nothing like that. I'm just really glad to be back in a situation where I understand everything. You wouldn't believe the day I fucking had."

"Does it have something to do," Ox-Head rumbles, circling behind me, "with the crocodile attached to your leg?"

"Eh?"

I peer down. Somehow during my initial self-appraisal, I had succeeded in completely overlooking the fact that I was, in no uncertain terms, hosting a stowaway.

From tail to snout, *this* specimen couldn't be more than four metres, a veritable twig beside the monster I'd grappled with. Its belly is comically round, swollen solid, a scaled balloon on which the rest of the reptile was unsteadily balanced, the creature wobbling with every gust of sulphuric breath. The limbs are vestigial, the eyes too; webbed with mucus, they might as well be decorative.

Noticing my attention, it rolls its gaze up. Tries to, at least, the whey-like substance glueing its corneas in place. But the rough panting noise that it makes isn't unfriendly, like a dog's greeting, eager but unsure.

Worms, whispers a sudden memory from when I hadn't given up on secondary school, when the biology teacher, who was tired of us running barefoot through the mud, soaking up hookworms and Guan Yin knows what, coerced us into watching a documentary about parasites. *Tapeworms, given an ounce of a chance, will multiply until there is no room and they have to eat through the intestinal walls, find somewhere else to fester.*

I stare at the crocodile still latched to my calf and wonder if I'd notice if it passed on the infection to me.

"What the fuck is that?"

Neither Ox-Head nor Horse-Face debase themselves with an answer. They stare, stonily, their heads cocked, ears twitching with more emotion than their muzzles could or would communicate, those ears

"Seriously, what the *fuck* is that?" I jab a finger at the thing.

"A god," intones a fresh voice, a quiet voice, a voice we all know.

In concert, the three of us go to our knees, kowtowing without resentment in the presence of Meng Po, Lady of Forgetfulness. She smells as she always does of the tisane she pours for the dead who have paid their dues, those prepared to revisit the karmic wheel. A medicinal bitterness, an attar that puts to mind liquorice and the sweet ginseng soup in which the yearly serving of tang yuan might float.

"Lady," I whisper.

"Lady," says Horse-Face.

"Lady," says Ox-Head and there is an ache there, a tremble of worship.

"Rise."

We obey.

Meng Po, you'd think, would aspire to opulence, cream-pale jade in the stitchings of her sleeves, gold threads for her robes. No reason to pauper yourself of excess when you sit at the apex of a pantheon, the flow of worshippers contingent on your favour. If Meng Po willed it, no one would leave and those who escaped Diyu would be worthless to the gods, their souls annihilated by the memory of torture. Yet despite that, Meng Po upholds a bewildering austerity, her only vanity an insistence that her chignon is perfect as the silver of a priest's cross. Without exception, she is only ever glimpsed in peasant garb of deepest ink, woven of rough wool.

Once, I asked her why. Meng Po had said it was so that the dead will not be surprised by how quickly old will come again.

"He was a god once. When the world was kinder to both itself and the ideas it worshipped." She hobbles to me, stooping to stretch a hand to the apparition. To my bewilderment, it nuzzles its snout into her open palm.

"Begging your pardon, lady, but I'm pretty sure that isn't Sobek. The Lord of Crocodiles, last I saw of him, was alive and possessed of a hearty appetite."

Meng Po shakes her head, scratching a path from the creature's nostrils up to the ridges that frame its sightless eyes. Unperturbed, it continues to croon. "That thing you saw wasn't Sobek."

"Sure looked like a giant crocodile god."

"Manners, Rupert, or I will make a necklace of your bones." Ox-Head lets it be known that he does not appreciate my impertinence by pincering my head between two colossal fingers. I've wondered for a while if he might be sweet on the old woman. Age is no factor among immortals, after all. And though the compulsion to wisecrack does stir, Ox-Head's application of pressure on my temples is more than sufficient to neuter it.

I swallow instead. "Got it."

"Perhaps I should be more clear. It *was* Sobek. Now, it is a husk, emptied by whatever it was that had taken root in its flesh, the last remnants of the god evicted and sent down here with you."

"Wait. Why? What's the point? Are the Egyptians working together with whatever the hell—ow, ow, ow, Guan Yin save me from your besotted ass, you stupid—*ow*."

"I worry sometimes that my speech is too anachronistic for this epoch. You keep misunderstanding me." Meng Po brings her head down, presses her mouth to the brow of the crocodile, a gesture so tender that I find myself inexplicably lonely for a mother whose face I no longer recall. That we might all meet our ends this way, safe in death's care, secure in the thought there would be no more pain. I envy him. "Let me rephrase. He is not here for any nefarious reasons. He is here to die."

"But—"

"When you perished, he saw his opportunity. He fled."

The crocodile warbles without ceasing, needing no breath, wanting no air, wanting nothing but Meng Po's love. I can almost forgive him his transgressions against me now.

"From what?"

Meng Po sighs. "If you have not figured it out yet, you shall."

Ordinarily, I like to think of myself as a reasonably smart man. Quick on his feet, quicker with the comebacks. Slightly deficient in the 'knowing when to keep my mouth shut' category, but no one is without their inadequacies. However, the effect of being slingshotted from quasi-normal to dead-by-crocodilian-dismemberment is something that takes a toll on a guy. Especially when the epilogue involves an angry mountain of livestock threatening to pulp your head like a berry. So, instead of saying something pithy, I add, "Bwuh?"

Before I can redeem myself, a familiar sensation hooks itself around the base of my sternum. A tugging, cold as a palmful of dry ice, before it snaps through my breastbone, and life drags me back, upwards, through the laminae of realities, all the worlds in between blurred into neon glare. There are fewer experiences more beautiful than this: the universe running through your fingers, every colour of what-is and what-could-be like a breath of pure hope, uncut, pristine, without even the faintest varnish of cynicism.

But Jesus on a jet plane does it *hurt* like a motherfucker.

FIVE

I WAKE UP on a mattress of crocodile guts, a whining noise in my ears, the air already jewelled with bumblebee-sized black flies who cannot believe their luck. That I'm here, sitting atop a mound of carrion like an unfortunate cake topper, is no issue to them: they wiggle into my ears, try their luck up my nostrils, cling to my lips. Their bodies are that strange kind of soft where you know, if you pinch them between your fingers, they won't burst but pulp, smearing marmalade-like over your skin.

That is, of course, the exact moment when my lungs decide they need to breathe.

My mouth crowd with flies, their legs and their wings everywhere, fluttering against the roof of my mouth, around the bend of my gums; they clump around my uvula and my tongue goes up as I gag. My throat seizes. I twist sideways and retch, vomiting a shallow bilious soup, pebbled with half-drowned insects. The worst thing about it is that it tastes better coming back up.

"Hi."

In the fugue that follows every resurrection, I'd somehow missed the man standing in front of me. I blink. He appears to be carrying a small, motorized hand saw.

"Hey."

The flies billow upwards as he takes an uncertain step forward, one hand outstretched. I wipe my mouth on the back of a sleeve, grimace, then try again on a patch of bare skin which, though blood-soaked, is not flecked with torn intestinal tissue. He turns his palm upwards for my inspection, fingers slightly crooked. It's a nice gesture, frankly. Under different circumstances, I'd have clasped that outstretched hand and hauled myself onto my feet.

But as it stands, I'm enthroned on a mountain of offal and the man, who has yet to identify himself in any meaningful way, is carrying a hand saw. Logic suggests that he was the one who freed me from the effluvium, but nice things don't happen when your name is Rupert Wong. If I've ever been saved for anything, it's for supper.

"I don't want to sound ungrateful, but what the fuck just happened here?"

"I... uh, I cut you out of a giant crocodile?"

"Yes, but *why*?"

He pauses. "Because Amanda asked me to?"

"Oh. Well. Okay, then." I take his hand in mine and let him pull me upright, a Chaplin-esque process that involves him skidding forward on the grass, a pancreas exploding under the weight of my palm as I crowbar myself into verticality, and the flies deciding, despite initial appearances, that we are, in fact, eminently edible. The last is a particularly interesting problem.

"Ow, fuck, *ow*—"

"Will you watch where you're swinging that thing?"

Abashed, my unnamed rescuer powers down his hand saw, and we resume our exodus post-haste, slapping at the flies, our skin already bubbling with bites. Luckily for us, the picnic spread of a thirteen-feet-long corpse is too enticing to ignore. The flies lose interest and we escape, panting, onto a lawn miraculously unoccupied save by a colony of fat, slightly furtive brown hares.

"So," I begin, scratching vigorously between my shoulderblades.

"So?"

"So."

He stares at me, befuddled. Ignoring the fact he just disembowelled a crocodile to save me, the man's not exactly what anyone would call hero material. The baby blue button-down, the khakis, even the white tennis shoes: it all contributes to an image, one that can only be captioned with the word *DAD* in block letters. Preferably in crayon, too. The fact that Amanda told him, of all people, to come procure me means one of the two things. Either the Internet couldn't care less if I survived to my next status update, or this is—

"*You're* Cason."

"Yes?"

"You. You're Cason."

"Yes? I—were you expecting somebody else?"

"Wait. Wait. *You're* the half-human son of the Devil that Amanda and Fitz have been talking you? *You.*" I look him over again. I guess I can see it. Upon second round of perusal, I realize the dad bod's as much camouflage as the wardrobe. What extraneous weight he has is laddered over a boxer's physique. One that has spent a few seasons on the bench, sure, but you can see the potential in the cabled shoulders, the oversized forearms. I massage my chin, frowning with escalating intensity.

"I'm beginning to feel like I should be getting offended by this. You know, my wife—"

"No, it's just"—I fumble for diplomacy and fail—"you're a lot less intimidating than I'd expected. Wait. What about your wife?

"She had some excellent ideas about why we do what we do."

"What exactly?"

"Cut down the other party. Wisecrack. We're scared."

I look our surroundings over. "In fairness, this seems like a good environment for that."

"Yeah. That's fair. Also, what the fuck?"

"I think you're supposed to say thank you."

"Look, you expect knights in shining armor. Not dads in white tennis shoes."

"Well. Polka dot."

"What do you—" I study the new patterns on his shoes. "Oh. Right. Er. Hope they didn't cost too much."

"Actually, it might be more of a Pollack."

"Okay, I'm sorry."

"It's kinda impressionist. Picasso in red?"

"I said I'm sorry!"

Cason shrugs a shoulder. A few scraps of white

cloud tumbleweed across the technicolour blue of the Florida sky, driven by a breeze that smells faintly of swamp. "Anyway, that isn't technically correct. What Amanda and Fitz said. I actually don't know what the exact percentage is, to be honest: Lucifer said he was my grandfather, but in that ambiguous 'I've spent eons debauching virgins' sort of way, and Cernunnos is absolutely a god, and my father. So, I guess it has to be at least somewhat less than half human."

"Oh. My. God."

"That would be my father, yes. And only if you're a neo-pagan. I don't like assuming." When I fail to laugh, he palms the back of his neck and chuckles nervously. "Sorry, sorry. I was just trying to make a joke—are you okay?"

"You make dad jokes." I wheeze, doubling over in slow-motion, a hand flapped in his general direction. I know I'm making a sound like a live rabbit being fed through a grinder, a hitching, high-pitched splutter that has to be disconcerting to hear, but there is only so much surrealism that a man can take before he breaks. Give me gore. Give me gods. Give me a firmament glazed in kicap manis and garnished with guts. Anything but this.

"I *am* a dad."

"Of *course* you are!"

"Seriously, should we get you a doctor or something?"

I unfold so fast that I splatter Cason with bilious run-off. He flinches away, one eye scrunched against the blood now dripping from his brow.

"What the hell is going on here? Amanda said you couldn't deal with sharing a room. I thought—I thought—you know, I'm not sure exactly *what* I think anymore. You just hacked me out of a crocodile. I'm not a good judge of normal. You tell me what's going on."

Cason spends a few seconds patting himself down before, with great deliberation, drawing a square of plaid cloth from a pocket. Miraculously, it is still pristine. He hands it to me.

"Look, I'm forty-two. I've got a real job, two kids. It's just a question of standards. I mean, I'm sure you're all nice people, but I'm too old to be doing the college dormitory bullshit."

I put my face in my hands. It's something I immediately regret, but not as much I might have without Cason's kind donation of a handkerchief. The thin cloth soaks up an impressive film of offal, before that familiar sourness pricks at my nose again. "Guan Yin save me, I'm going to die. This is the end. These goddamned ang mohs—"

"Are you really sure you don't need a doctor?"

"Probably do," I pant, shambling over to Cason so I can drape an arm around his shoulder. He winces as

I crush him to my side, his head jammed between my shoulder and the edge of my jaw. "But you know what I want? What I really, *really* want?"

"A zig-a-zig-bath?"

"We're either going to kill each other or be good friends. You know that, right?"

"Yup."

WE RETURN TO the Best Western, squelching, a pair of bedraggled uncles in sodden clothes, having hosed down on the way back. Fortunately, we're in Orlando, so no one gives us anything but a wide berth. Disneyland, after all, is a holy land for middle-aged hopefuls desperate to see if a pilgrimage to the happiest place in the world might restore their enthusiasm for life and possibly, wanton yet predictable and responsible sex. Which is to say, more than a few guests have likely come into the lobby drunk as skunks and drenched from the local water park.

Cason and I file into the elevator, and I lean against the rail as the doors close and we begin to climb.

"What's in this for you?" I ask.

He stows a last-generation iPhone into a pocket and rucks his brow. "This whole debacle? I don't know. The usual, I suppose."

"Fame? Fortune? Access to all the female bodies you can hope for? Other nice things beginning with the letter F?" I tick off possibilities on my fingers.

"Yeah," Cason interrupts, voice quiet. "Family and future, specifically. You know, for a long time, I thought I'd never do"—a flutter of a hand—"this bullshit again, but as it turns out, it takes exactly two minutes of conversation to change my mind."

"What was their sales pitch?"

"If we fail to save the world, my family will be horribly devoured by forces too terrible to comprehend?" Cason tilts his head. "You know. That sort of thing."

"Yeah. Okay. Sorry." I study our shoes. Pink water still drips from the soles, a reminder of our recent adventures. "God, I'm really bad at small talk. Shouting cheap bravado in the face of danger? Sure. But actually talking to a human being. Man…

"You're in good company. I think it's easy to laugh in the face of danger because it doesn't care. But when you're being evaluated—"

"Judged."

"Observed for acceptable human behaviour. That's just hard." Cason sighs. His eyes skate to the mirrored wall behind me, possibly taking note of my expanding bald spot. "You have any kids?"

"Had a kid. Buried him last year."

Cason's expression is stricken. "I'm so sorry—"

"No, no, no." I throw my hands up, trying to negate any further expression of sympathy. I won't lie and say I hadn't grown attached to George. You love your partner's children, even if they're skinless horrors, unable to sustain themselves on anything but blood from a freshly opened vein. Nonetheless, there's only so much despair you can muster when you know someone is, without question, in a better place. "It's fine. He was dead already."

"What?"

"What?"

In the horrified silence that follows, I realize the immensity of what I'd said and palm the back of my neck, staring down again at our waterlogged footwear.

"That probably needed some context. Let's see. Ah, my ex-partner's child from their last marriage was an undead monster who I had to bury once the life fled from them."

Cason's eyes dilate infinitesimally. "Is that your way of saying that you killed the—"

"No. Yes. Maybe. Depends. Technically, I was responsible for George's death. And Minah's death, but no, *Jesus,* not like that—" I start forward as Cason recoils, his repulsion blatant. "It was... complicated."

"I'm sure Ted Bundy probably said the same thing." Cason looks me over. His brows crook upwards. "Listen, I'm not here to judge. We're just colleagues.

What you do on your own time isn't my problem right now."

I consider my options. On one hand, it'd be nice to build our professional relationship on something other than a bedrock of justified distrust. Cason already has reason to feel awkward in my presence: vivisection involves breaking bones, not ice. And Guan Yin knows what he saw in Sobek's flayed belly. No one has ever explained to me the precise science of resurrection. It's possible that I pop back into existence, fully formed, limbs and ligament restored. But more likely than not, it involves traumatising amounts of body horror, the kind that, if documented, would win every award for special effects imaginable.

On the other hand, it isn't as though I had a particularly virtuous youth. I've beaten, battered, bruised, bludgeoned, broken and brutalized so many people, done so many things that are, in the most literal sense of the word, terrible, it isn't factually incorrect to see me as a bad person. So what if Cason decides this because of a misconception? He'd still be right.

And more crucially, it'd take me time to fully explain what had happened, time to discuss who Minah was, what she meant to be, why I'd bartered with a dragon god for her ability to escape the karmic cycle.

Nonetheless—

"Hey, it's not like you can talk."

Cason stares at me. "Sorry?"

"You're the grandson of the Devil." I shove my hands into my pockets and shrug.

"Just because my parentage is mildly diabolical. Also, weren't you the one going off on how impossible—"

"*Mildly?* Do we need to go into a discussion about what the Devil is, precisely? Because last time I checked, he isn't just 'mildly' diabolical, he is literally—"

A soft *ding* interrupts the stand-off. The elevator doors rattle open, revealing a clutch of Scandinavian tourists, sheepishly huddled to one side of the cramped passage. To a man, they're all wearing 'I <3 Disneyland' shirts. Their gazes trace a route from our faces to the pink puddles spreading under our feet.

"Pool party," I declare with sudden enthusiasm. "Lots of bottles of wine in the pool. American tradition."

Cason fixes me with an incredulous look. "Whiskey tango *fuck*-trot."

"Very exclusive American thing," I continue, aware that mendacity isn't strictly required but just in case, it wouldn't hurt to have a cogent narrative, however improbable it might be. "You might get lucky and be invited to one of these events."

All attention, mine included, pivots then to Cason. The Nordic delegation—who could well be a family, but I'm not about to assume anyone who looks the same is necessarily related, even if turnabout's amusing play—tack on encouraging smiles.

"Yeah." Cason draws out the vowels, his answering grin sickly. "What he said."

I direct finger-guns at anyone who will make eye contact, sidling out of the elevator as I do, Cason letting loose a tired groan behind me. "Awesome. Yeah. Okay. Let's go! Enjoy Disneyland. Woohoo!

"You're a fucking idiot," Cason stage-whispers as the doors close behind us, drawing up lateral to my right shoulder.

I shrug. "I get that a lot."

SIX

"You're shorter than you looked in pictures," Fitz announces from his perch at the windowsill, a leg drawn to his chest, the other held straight, heel anchored on the musty carpet.

Best Western tries, it really does; but the turnover for this place must be absurd. There is an exhausted jocularity to the room that puts to mind kindergarten teachers, or fast food mascots on the brink of a psychotic break. The walls are an irradiated shade of bile, the valances are faux red velvet, the flooring is redolent of pine, and the white paint on the ceiling is considerably fresher than the smoke-tinged bedsheets. Amanda and Fitz have every light turned on and the windows open, letting in the noon-light.

"How long was I dead?"

Every head turns again in my direction.

"Sorry. I wasn't trying to make this about me. I was just wondering if anyone knew. " I stoop and crook a finger through a cabinet handle, tugging it open. Jackpot. The mini-bar, like everything else about our accommodations, is comfortably mediocre. I pry a miniature bottle of Jack Daniels from the selection and pour the contents into a styrofoam cup.

Amanda blinks slowly. For reasons best undeciphered, she'd sloughed her original outfit for a variant of what Fitz and I are wearing: Hawaiian shirt, sandals, shorts belted high. If a stranger walked in, they'd probably decide we were the detritus of a once-famous musical ensemble, now reduced to the status of a cover band, and Cason our down-on-his-luck manager, disgraced and dismissed, desperate to make us his redemption.

"Eight hours. Give or take," she declares, at last. "Depending on how closely Sobek's digestive system mirrors that of a real crocodile's."

I drain my cup in one go. "You are definitely being too casual about this."

Amanda shrugs, and after a moment, I do the same. While I'm rummaging for ingredients to make a proper cocktail, having decided that decorum has no place the day after coming back from the dead, Cason walks over to one of the two beds and seats himself. Springs creak and he frowns. "You're exactly what I pictured."

"Underfed crackhead?" Fitz opens the window, leans out as he produces another hand-rolled cigarette from his person.

"Something like that." Despite assurances that he would not show me any bigotry, Cason's still clearly experiencing some doubts about my proximity. He stares in my direction, a cool look, before he nods at the fridge. "Got a beer in there, *friend?*"

I lob a can of Pabst at him. "We gotta talk about what I said in the elevator."

"Like I said, not my business." He snatches the beer from the air, pops the tab in a quick motion, tilting the foaming mouth away.

"What's he talking about?" Fitz cranes an eyebrow. He ignites the tip of his cigarette and drapes out of the window, the fingers of his free hand anchored in the frame. He sucks at the smoke and blows out, a curl of smoke wafting skyward.

"He murdered his wife and kid."

"Definitely the wrong interpretation of what was

an incredibly nuanced situation." I mix ginger ale and dime-store gin, feeling slightly, as I do, like I've disappointed the universe in a profound way. "But maybe right now's not the time to get into it."

"He's right," Amanda says and the air blues at the sound of her voice, crystallizing, so the world is suddenly in high-definition, every colour rendered so sharply it hurts the eyes. Reality fissures, just enough to see between its laminae: Amanda is raw electricity, a murmuration of data points, impossible, indecipherable. I blink. The effect fades away. "This is where it gets real. Now that we have the three of you collected, there's one more person to find. Ironically, she's in a domestic partnership with someone I've known for an incredibly long time."

Fitz pushes from the windowsill and pads forward, a thumb hooked in the pocket of his shorts. At the last minute, he flicks his cigarette out of the window. "You didn't tell me that."

"I didn't think it was necessary to mention. Naree and I are old friends. The details are unimportant."

Cason takes a loud slug of his beer. "I don't want to be rude, but my youngest just pulled off a grand slam at the tee-ball all-stars, and if I'm going to be missing important life events, I want it to be for a good reason. Could we possibly get on with this?"

"I—" Amanda collects the tip of her ponytail in a

hand and begins twirling the end around a finger, her agitation girlish and disconcertingly out-of-character. As with so many other things about Amanda, it seems put on: hyperreal, yet disconnected from the usual portraiture of her psyche. But then again, that could also be a miscategorisation of her character. What *is* the Internet, after all, but a museum of memetic ideas collated at seeming random? "It's complicated."

"That is so not an answer," Fitz says.

"It is absolutely an answer," Amanda counters, dusting herself off. "It just isn't the answer you wanted."

OUR DESTINATION REVEALS itself to be the University of Florida, a reasonably impressive aggregation of structures which Cason quickly dismisses.

"Apparently, it's all about the Greek life here," he confides sourly, as we cross into the campus grounds. It is closing on dusk when we arrive. The sky has burned itself down to indigo, and the light is shrunken to blooms of pink. Apparently, we'll be accosting our target at her last class of the day, although no one will tell me whether the quarry's a student, a teacher, a janitor, or a nightmare creature folded into the rafters, unable to escape until the school closes for the night. Of course, that part's my own fault; they already *did* tell me and I missed it. I really need to learn to talk less and listen more.

"I have no idea what that means." I look past Cason's shoulders to the manicured lawns, the attractive topiary, the students drifting between buildings. A few of them are dragging six-packs of beer.

"It's a party school. My eldest was hoping we'd let him come here to study, but no. He's going somewhere like CalTech. We're not letting him waste his youth."

Cason follows my attention to where a group of students is canvassing passers-by for donations. From this distance, I can't tell what cause they've aligned themselves with. The gilded sign is an abomination of curlicues and complicated lettering.

"Where'd you go to school?" he asks.

I don't miss a beat. "Hard knocks."

Cason laughs, loudly and without apology, but he doesn't say anything more. Instead, we leg it into a brick-red edifice and move rapidly towards a set of double doors. No one but the janitorial staff spare us any attention, and even that seems cursory.

"Computer geeks," Fitz whispers.

"Come on." Amanda glances down at a watch that I know doesn't work. "Naree should be just about done teaching."

We enter a white-walled amphitheatre, bowl-shaped and ribbed with chairs, staircases on either end. Students crowd the seats: most in hoodies, battered laptops on display. It's a young crowd, but it isn't their youth that makes them unique. It's the fact that more than half of them are not Caucasian, but an eclectic mix of other ethnicities; a sight that makes me indescribably happy. Nothing like seeing non-white kids rocking through the education system. That said, they *do* share an intensity, which testifies to either an uncommon intellect or a rare respect for their lecturer. Fitz gestures us towards the wall, and we huddle together in a queue. In minutes, it becomes clear where said educator falls on that spectrum.

Smart people are everywhere. Men and women for whom physics is a puzzlebox to crack between their teeth and mathematics is a provocation, something to reach into, bleed on, reconfigure with a pricking of their thumbs, so that two plus two is the colour of a dead woman's eyes. But not all of them can humanise these theorems, can discuss quantum as easily as an episode of a mid-list sitcom, and even fewer exude the kind of charisma radiating from the locus of the class.

Naree is a *presence*.

Short, gorgeous, fat, Korean, she paces the floor beside her whiteboard with obvious excitement. Her clothes have an anti-authoritarian lean: punk with a ghost of goth in the latex thigh-highs she wears, stars and moons emblazoned on the black. Naree talks with her hands, with metaphors both esoteric and earthy, with all of her being, acting out every analogy with dizzying enthusiasm.

I peel from my corner of the wall and sidle up to Amanda, leaning over, an arm crossed over my chest. "So, here's my question: why exactly do you need us as back-up?"

"I told you—"

"Did you get her pregnant?"

"What."

"I don't know. It's possible. Some people seem to really enjoy the internet."

Amanda stares at me like I've sprouted a number of extraneous heads. "I can't tell if you're joking, sometimes."

"I can't either." I shrug. "But in all seriousness, what is the story here?"

"If I tell you, will you go away?"

"Yes."

"Liar."

"Worth a try."

The class ends without incident. Students funnel from their seats towards Naree. In minutes, she is ringed by a crowd three bodies deep, every last one of them with questions, papers, excuses for extensions to one assignment or another. We wait until the commotion simmers to a dull clamour before wading into the throng, Naree still oblivious to our arrival. It isn't until Amanda, squeezing between two blond boys in matching letter jackets, touches Naree on the wrist that she finally takes notice.

"Amanda?" Eyes, lids heavy with shimmering green-golds, widen. "Oh. Em. Gee. It really is you. I can't believe it. You're here. You're *actually* here."

Naree burrows through the crowd and into Amanda's arms, squealing, her next words buried against the other woman's rib cage. It takes a moment for her exhilaration to be reciprocated, Amanda's face cycling between expressions before at last settling on a peculiar species of relief. Slowly, she folds her arms around Naree's shoulders, one after the other.

"Hey," she says, soft enough that we almost do not hear.

At that, Naree pries herself out of Amanda's embrace. The students begin an awkward exodus, unable to make sense of our presence. A few bob their chins in our directions, a few scowling in disapproval. Most ignore the fact we're there, their attention lingering on Naree, and it takes her outright dismissing them for the dregs of the class to finally disperse.

"You're kinda popular," Fitz offers, raking a hand through his hair.

"Eh." Naree loops an arm around Amanda's and squeezes her hand, a sororal gesture. "I think they just like the fact I'm not sixty-five and white. Anyway. I'm Naree. I guess you're Amanda's questing party."

"Guilty as charged," says Fitz.

Cason extends a hand, his smile warm if mildly uncertain of itself. "Cason."

"Rupert," I announce, completing the triptych of introductions.

Naree shakes our hands in turn, her grip firm, her gaze steady and fearless. When we're done with the formalities, Naree takes a step back, exhaling as she does. "Tanis doesn't know yet."

"I thought not," Amanda says, tone even. "It isn't your responsibility to tell her."

"That... no, that's not why. Although I'm still trying to figure out how to tell her that we're talking again. Tanis knows why we stopped being, uh, *friends* the first time." Naree gives a helpless shrug before flitting to her desk, where she extracts a battered leather satchel from under the surface and drapes it over a shoulder. "And after everything that happened in the last year or so, I wasn't sure if I wanted to spring any surprises on her. I mean, Bee was already *a lot*, you know what I'm saying?"

"Bee?" Cason asks.

"Beatrice. Our baby. We named her for one of Tanis' sisters who, sadly, isn't around anymore." The brightness wicks from Naree's face, her smile faltering as her eyes drop, memory clouding her expression. But she perks up quickly enough. "She was incredible, though. You guys would have loved her."

"I'm sure." Cason hesitates. "Do you have any pictures of Beatrice?"

"The kiddo or her namesake? Because I actually do have both." Naree waggles her eyebrows dramatically, two fingers already on the clasp of her bag.

I cut in before the photos come out. "Actually, I'm really curious about that thing you just said. Why *did* you and Amanda stop talking the first time?"

"Oh. That? You didn't tell them?" Naree looks at Amanda, purses her mouth.

"It didn't come up."

"*Liar*." I jab a finger at Amanda.

"Yes. But it can wait. Let's not forget exactly why we're all here. Personal histories can wait."

Any impulse to continue with the teasing dies at the sight of Amanda's expression, her face haunted, her mouth drawn to a tense line. I wince. It has been easy, too easy, to buy into the camaraderie, the levity of that connection, of coaxing loose a reluctant answer. Like we're nothing but schoolyard kids and this isn't the end of the world. Heat blotches my face. I poke my tongue against the inside of a cheek, sigh.

A silence drifts through the room, lingering until I break it with a soft, "Sorry."

"Whatever." Amanda smoothes away her unease, recovering her original façade, features once again without anything but a bland pleasantness; the timbre of her voice civil, absent of significant emotion. "We should get going. If that is okay with you, Naree?"

"Yeah. We just have to make one stop."

"Fine," says Amanda. "And where's that?"

The smile is incandescent, almost confrontational. "Daycare. It's my turn to pick up Bee, and I guess y'all are coming with me."

SEVEN

HAVE YOU HEARD the one where the Devil's grandson, a prophet, and a tourist walk into a daycare centre in Florida? It begins with the three of them discussing contingency plans in the event that the children, being more perspicacious than adults, take offence at their existence, and it ends with them wading through an excited sea of bright-eyed kids, their calves suddenly commandeered by ecstatically shrieking toddlers.

"Why aren't they *scared?*" Fitz hisses as he plucks a little Hispanic girl from his knee, holding her out at arm's length, while she screams for him to toss her in the air.

"I blame Cason."

Of the three of us, Cason is the only one who appears at peace with the scenario. He has a child draped over his back, their arms around his neck, and one riding on the crook of each elbow. Cason, for some reason, is also having an animated conversation with their warden, a sweet-faced redhead in bohemian attire, the airy wardrobe at odds with the distress cragged into her brow.

Fitz sets down the girl. "I blame Naree."

"Speaking of Naree, where the hell is she?"

As though they'd been waiting their whole lives for the opportunity, listening for the moment that an adult might trip, a chorus of childish voices immediately belt out the word 'hell' like it's a nursery rhyme, sing-songing the expletive at increasing volumes, their glee escalating with every exclamation of the word.

"Shit."

Just as quickly, the choir picks up on the new obscenity, and the air rings with words both fecal and infernal. Adding insult to injurious guilt, the children suddenly link arms and begin dancing in circles around us.

"Class! Please! That isn't a word that we use. It is a no-no word—"

"Shit!"

"Hell!"

I lean over to Fitz, who is already being harangued by two sets of twins, his body the rope in an impromptu game of tug-of-war. As he see-saws one way and the other, I declare, "You know, their teacher is probably going to kill us."

"No sssh—" Fitz swallows the word before he finishes it. "Again. Where the fuck is Naree? Oh, Mary dick-sucking Louise—"

If I wasn't already consigned to the bureaucracy of the Ten Chinese Hells, I imagine this would be the deed that tips me over the edge into eternal damnation. As the aftershocks of Fitz's reflexive swearing spreads, cherubic faces becoming illuminated with new, forbidden knowledge, I start cackling. When messiahs of manure are invoked in giddy earnest, I succumb to guffaws, burying my face in my hands, even as the kindergarten teacher barrels down on Fitz, no longer a paragon of pacifism, but an advancing seraph, full of righteous fury and tiny wildflowers in her braids.

"Come on, this isn't the first time someone's cussed in front of these kids—"

"How dare you." She delivers the words like a prophecy, the syllables given the weight of worlds. I sidestep as she speeds up, but apparently there's no real cause for alarm. Fitz, for now, is the sole recipient of her ire. Briefly, the woman pauses, practically wobbling in place, and in a more normal voice breathlessly demands, "And which of these unfortunate children belong to you, anyway? I don't think I've ever seen you—"

"None of them, actually."

"*Pervert.*"

He dances away, palms raised. "That is… okay, not a *completely* accurate—"

"Not helping your case, Fitz," I shoot at him as I cross the vestibule to safer grounds, migrating to where Cason is standing with a look of perfect dismay.

"What did you two *do?*" he asks.

Loyal to comedic timing, the kids pick this instance to revitalise their rendition of *shit, fuck, goddamn,* and other blasphemies first popularized in the sixteenth century. I jab a thumb in their direction. "Improved their education."

"Jesus, Rupert, they're three years old—"

And Naree elects *that* moment to saunter out from a corner office, leading a pint-sized replica of herself by the hand. The obscene choir halts, takes a breath, then renews their felonious worship. Two things happen as the first 'fuck' hits the air: Fitz dodges a blow from the kindergarten teacher and Naree slaps palms over her child's ears, mouthing *what the heck is going on* as she does. I shrug and point at the gate.

"Exit, stage anywhere?" I say.

"You idiots need to find me a new pre-preschool for Beatrice," Naree hisses, scooping her daughter up, and stalking towards the gate.

I follow in lockstep. Fitz jogs after us and Cason lags behind, apparently intent on smoothing things over with the harassed educator. "Deal."

"And smooth things over with this school! If this blows up, that's it. Bee's going to be a social pariah. People will talk." She accelerates.

I flutter a hand at Cason, who is still talking to the woman. "Already being dealt with."

"And—"

"Yeah?"

"And—"

Naree slows as we round the corner. She's parked under an enormous magnolia tree, its boughs lousy with white flowers. A breeze picks up and petals wick from the branches, suddenly sleeting down upon us. Naree straps Beatrice into her appointed seat in the back, imperiously gesturing at Fitz to take custody of the carrier, and straightens to regard me over the rim of her car's roof.

"Yeah?"

"That was funny." Shutting the passenger door with a quiet click, Naree flashes a megawatt smile. "But don't ever tell anyone that I said that."

"Got it."

"Cool. Now let's go home."

HOME, AS IT turns out, is a single-storey house made of cardboard.

"Is this in any way *safe?*"

I gawk at the building, mildly dismayed, half-out of the car window, torso propped up by an elbow jammed against the side of the car door. The walls are yellow, flimsy as a politician's campaign promise; the roof is white, erratically shingled; there's a single cupola slanting from what is possibly the attic, or a questionable attempt at adding value to low-cost housing. But the lawn is green and well-tended, the rose bushes flushed, and the light pouring from the sliding glass doors is the warm gold of good custard.

"What do you mean is it safe?" Naree evacuates her daughter from the backseat while the rest of us extract ourselves. "Of course it's safe. It's a house."

"That's not a house."

"No, that's definitely a house."

"A house is made of bricks. This is made of *cardboard.*" I retort. "You could drive a car through that."

Naree's brows ruck, ridging the corners of her eyes. She ushers Bee into Cason's custody, the latter already so charmed with the girl that they're devising little stories, fables dense with what I can only hope are the names of Bee's plush animals. Otherwise, well, Cason owes us an explanation about the depths of his personal depravities. Whatever Mr. Rubber Rainbow is, it can't be good if it sprung full-grown from an adult man's subconscious. Fitz yawns and stretches as he unfolds from the car.

"The houses in Malaysia look like Alcatraz," he offers, mildly.

"Really." Naree makes a moue of her mouth, tapping a finger against her lips, beringed with a key chain. "I guess that explains—"

"That is patently untrue." I close the door behind me and lean back against the car, looking up at the house, the land surrounding it. To date, no one has, in any meaningful fashion, explained who or what Tanis is. It stands to reason that she is as preternaturally gifted as we are. I wonder, though; why is Amanda so dead set on back-up? More important yet, where on the earth *is* she?

"Your houses look like *prisons*," Fitz shoots.

"Our houses are built to stand monsoons."

"Monsoons, prison breaks, what's the difference?" His levity stutters as he says this, expression shuttering: diluted and then drained entirely by whatever memory his words conjured.

Naree goes immediately for compassion: an arm unfurls, ready to clasp Fitz in an embrace, but she stops at the precipice of being too familiar and her hand closes. She shrinks back, fist pressed to her mouth, face submerged in thought. Before I can meddle, voice reassurance or encouragement to either parties, Naree does a one-eighty and explodes forward, flings both arms around Fitz.

Although not in any way respectful of personal space, it does its job. Fitz ricochets out of his reverie, yipping as Naree's embrace constricts. "Hey, what— ow, geeze, you've got a grip."

"I've been doing Brazilian Jiu Jitsu," Naree announces with unconvincing haughtiness, nose tipped back. "Tanis is a complete bad-donkey, so I've—"

"Bad what?" Fitz and I say in unison.

"It's parent speak for a very tough person." Cason looks up from where he's supervising Bee's attempt at chalking hopscotch squares into the driveway. "You know. Donkey. As in, another word for."

Naree twirls her hand. "Standard precautions against the sort of you-know-what that just happened you-know-where."

"Haven't forgiven us yet, huh?" says Fitz.

She lets go. "Nope."

We are about to enter the house when a tall woman slinks out of the gloom, her fingers embedded in Amanda's collar, who she's holding up like a disobedient kitten. The new arrival is tendons and teeth, black leather and a walk that *clinks* each time her heel hits the pavement, revolver and knives and Guan-Yin-knows-what-else bouncing against her lean hip. In contrast with everything else, the woman's soft halo of short dark curls seems out of place, like a scrap of lambswool the wolf decided to convert into whimsical millinery. "She says she knows you."

"You must be Tanis." I take an automatic step back as her gaze passes over my face, hands held up placatingly. Her eyes chill infinitesimally when they take notice.

"You must be Naree's friends. If you're not..." She glances at Naree, still folded around Fitz. "Babe. Nod once if this is a scenario that you did not consent to, because—"

"No, no, no." Naree lets go and bounds over to Tanis, an arm hooked around the lankier woman's waist, her cheek laid against her ribcage. Despite the fact Tanis is still holding Amanda an inch above the ground without even a glazing of sweat, an act so natural Tanis might as well be a housewife modelling an empty tote bag for our inspection, the sweet domesticity of the sight isn't lost on me: Tanis and Naree belong together, a fit as perfect as the letters of the name of God. "They're the guests."

"Please tell me they're not staying."

"We're not staying," Amanda says glacially. "And will you put me down?"

"Listen. If you ever become a house-owner, you'd understand. Something about furtive strangers skulking around, looking for entry, just *gets* to you." Tanis releases Amanda, nonetheless. Just for the half of a second, I see her tongue flick out and lap at the air. "Especially if they're people like you."

"That's kinda racist," Fitz remarks from a safe distance.

"You are only here by grace of my partner." If looks could kill, Tanis would have us minced, seasoned, neatly pleated into little dumpling wrappers. "Don't push it."

"I'm just saying—"

"In that case, you need to stop talking." Tanis presses a kiss onto the apex of Naree's head, lingering there, face buried in the gleaming black mass of her hair, before exhaling noisily and peeling away. She drops to a knee beside Bee, both arms outstretched, and I watch as her expression gentles into love. Maybe that's all it takes when it comes to parents. One glimpse of their offspring and the walls come down, the swords are lowered, and—

"And you need to move away from my daughter before you regret it."

Maybe not.

Cason doesn't take the bait, omits the wisecracking, just duck-walks backwards with a gracious expression on his open face. "I totally understand that. I'd be the same if I saw a stranger keeping company with my kids. Especially at this age."

Tanis spreads her arms and Bee trundles into reach, cooing nonsense noises, like a contented dove. "Sorry, but I'm not really interested in bonding exercises."

"Come on, babe. They're guests."

"I get that they're guests. But it is also possible to—" Tanis stops herself, lifting Bee into her arms as she unfolds, and begins counting down from ten at a nearly inaudible volume. Naree giggles into a hand. "Let's just get everyone inside. Don't want the alligators eating up the tourists."

"Too late," I mutter, slouching past.

"We'll explain." Fitz twitches his shoulders and slopes along behind me.

The spell breaks; the standoff ends. As is always the case, it is irreverence that whittles the savage beast into aggrieved surrender. Tanis sucks at her teeth and then sighs the long-tormented sigh of a woman who'd given up on the world making sense.

"He actually did get eaten by an alligator," Cason notes.

"Crocodile," I correct.

"I didn't ask." Tanis sighs again but imparts no further comment.

Naree unlocks the front door and ushers us inside. Washed in the glow from the fairy-lights threaded across the door frames, the interior isn't big, but it is pleasant. There's a post-collegiate quality to the furnishings: IKEA couches, do-it-yourself shelving; a stack of books on quantum physics, the pile crowned by an unused ashtray. Potted shrubbery is everywhere, as well as hampers full of toys, a stray LEGO set, and Bee's artistic masterpieces: a spread of luridly crayoned papers depicting houses, stick figures, and what may well be the end of the world. You can never tell with kids.

But the hardwood surfaces gleam and the few antiques, carefully positioned out of reach of a child, look old as omens.

Still radiating cataclysmic quantities of resentment, Tanis marches Bee into one of the side rooms. Naree gazes after her partner, wags her head once, and meanders to the kitchen. The light in her expression switches back on as she beams at us.

"There's just about enough beer for two rounds, but if anyone wants more, they're going to need to hit up the gas station around the block." She hooks a finger through the empty ring of a six-pack, the cans tall and obsidian and gleaming. I don't recognize the label scorched onto their surface.

"Do they take credit?" Fitz sprawls over the two-seat couch.

Amanda seats herself opposite him on an armchair that is probably older than anything else in the room, a last-generation monstrosity of paisley and stuffing, its corners fretted, gnawed-down by a currently-absent cat. Cason tails Naree into the kitchen, only to be shooed back into the living room, the latter tsking as she pads back over with the beer,

"I'm not an ATM," Amanda says.

"You wound me. Do I look like the kind of guy who would take advantage of the fact you have, quite literally, a limitless capacity for rebalancing the books?"

"Do you really want an answer to that?"

Fitz cackles uproariously but adds nothing more.

Naree pops the tab of a can, perches herself on the armrest of Amanda's chair, looking at her with mild curiosity. "Can you really do that?"

Colour flutters onto Amanda's cheeks as she ducks her head, a tendril of hair smoothed behind an ear. "More or less. It really is more my brother's province than mine, but I have some control of the digital."

"'Some,'" Fitz says.

Amanda ignores him. "But I try to avoid tampering with the flow of the Internet as much as I can. It's an ecosystem delicate as any other. You can't just fuck with that. Not without consequence. These days…"

"Fake news," Naree declares.

"Exactly."

"I'm too old for this shit." I pinch the bridge of my nose and grab a beer.

Cason remarks, settling on a chair. "Age is a number."

"Don't start with the wise-dad shit."

A two-count of silence as we pass looks between each other. I crack open my beer and take a sip. The cold molasses-black brew tastes like chocolate and smells like a coffee shop, decadent almost to a fault.

"Anyway," says Fitz, between swallows of his beer. "We should probably get this show on the road."

"By that I assume you mean someone explaining what the fuck is going on." Tanis steps back into the room utterly silently. She shucks her leather jacket and drapes it over the hook on the door behind her, revealing an efficient frame, no excess in any direction, whether fat or muscle.

Her eyes make an orbit of our expectant faces. "Seriously. What the fuck is going on?"

"This is Amanda." Naree points at the woman beside her.

"Wait. Same Amanda that went Terminator on you ages back?"

"Terminator?" I say, in perfect unison with the rest.

"When Naree was about fifteen, she had a friend on the Internet. Someone named Amanda. Amanda was—correct me if I get any part of this wrong, babe—having a conversation with Naree one day, and suddenly, there was a disconnected printer spitting out papers full of the words *How do you like it?*" Her voice dips into something dangerous. "Then, it was Naree's phone, her TV, her DVD player. All screaming. 'How do you like it?'"

Silence unrolls over the room like police tape.

"Wow," says Fitz.

"Everyone had a rebellious phase," Cason says. "It's natural."

"I was young," Amanda says, before anyone else can speak, cheeks florid. The colour travels up her forehead and down in capillaries along her throat. She sits with both hands wrapped around her can of beer, seemingly mesmerized by a picture on the wall. "You do stupid things when you're trying to show off."

"What the fuck *are* you?" Tanis whispers.

"That's not important."

"What. The. *Fuck*. Are. You."

Naree withdraws from Amanda and skips backwards—three quick hops—into Tanis's proximity. As though on auto-pilot, the taller woman extends an arm and drapes it over Naree's shoulders. "You're...

the god of technology, aren't you? Something like that."

"The Internet," Amanda says, sotto voce. "I'm the Internet. At least, the part of me that created this body."

"What do you mean 'this bo—'"

"She's a clone." I stab a finger at Amanda. "The Internet makes clones that, I guess, are microchipped like cats? Because I don't know how else you download information into a brain. Sometimes, the clones get overloaded. Sometimes, they look different. And sometimes, they apparently blow up because there's too much input or something, and their intelligence is dependent on whether they have access to satellite signal? I don't actually understand the full specifics. But that is the general gist of it. Everyone caught up?"

There's an awkward silence.

"Please don't smite my credit record."

"There is nothing I can do to your credit record that you haven't already done to yourself."

"Fair." I evaluate the climate of the room. So far, no one has contradicted me, laughed, choked, supplied a snide comment, or even endeavoured to put a bullet through my head. This is an improvement on my usual situation. "Did I get all the facts right?"

"Eh." A seesaw motion of Amanda's hand.

"Good enough." I shrug, slamming back at least a quarter of my beer.

Meanwhile, Tanis has her forehead cushioned in her free hand.

"Okay," she says, sighing. "Okay. Fine. You're the Internet. You're—" Her eyes alight on each of us in turn.

"A prophet, for want of a better word," says Fitz.

"Grandson of the Devil," says Cason.

"I'm just a cook." When the weight of their combined scrutiny becomes too much, I hunch down into my shoulders, adding in a small voice, "Also, I can't stay dead and I worked for Hell."

"So," says Naree, pointing at Cason. "You worked for his granddad?"

"No. The Chinese Hells," I clarify. "There are a lot of hells. Which, in retrospect, is incredibly fitting given the direction our species is heading."

"We're moving away from the subject." Another sigh from Tanis, longer, louder than the first, less patient than the first batch. "Okay. So. We have the grandson of the Devil, the Internet, a prophet, and an undead cook—"

"I prefer the phrase 'reluctantly immortal.'"

"I'd prefer if you shut up, but we can't get everything we want."

"Touché."

"*Anyway*," says Tanis, pointing at us all with both hands, like an irate conductor conducting the cacophony of an ill-trained orchestra. "What the hell does any of this have to do with *me?*"

"You're the fourth part of the prophecy," says Fitz.

"Oh. *Great*. Prophecies. No." Tanis drops her arms and turns to walk out. "I'm done already. I'm not going to be part of any of this."

"I don't think we really have a choice here..." Fitz begins.

"There's always a choice. And my decision is to stay out of this—"

"You have a daughter." And I can't tell if it is a trick of Amanda's, or if the world itself is leaning into her words, but whatever is going on, the light seems to dim where Tanis isn't standing. The colours desaturate, melt. Only Tanis is in high-definition, speared by the attentions of fate itself. "If you don't come with us, you're condemning her to death. There won't *be* a future. There won't be a world."

"Bullshit. I know how prophecy works—"

"Because you ate the heart of Cassandra. We know. But you have to understand. Prophecy accounts for small variances, but certain aspects are immutable. In this case, we need your visions—"

"Wait. She ate what now?" I start.

"You can have them for free. How about that?"

Tanis inhales, about to pontificate on what she'd seen, only to interrupt herself. "Also, why the fuck do you need me when you already have an actual prophet?"

"Because the *Chronicler*," growls Amanda, "hears the words of the gods, but Cassandra was different. She wasn't intended to be a loudspeaker. She was a mistake. Cursed. What she saw, what she knew—it was meant to make her go mad."

"Again. *Bullshit* and completely irrelevant. I—"

"I have something to say."

All eyes go to Cason.

"Go ahead. Ignore the cook. The grandson of the Devil is much more important."

"I'm sure your contribution is important." Tanis digs the nail of her middle finger into her forehead and begins massaging slow circles into the skin. Naree pats her sympathetically on the shoulder. "Say whatever it is you need to say. Why don't we get a talking stick while we're at it? Make sure everyone has a turn."

"I—you know, that's kind of offensive, but we can come back to that—I just wanted to point out that this isn't about the world. I can understand not wanting to give a damn about strangers. I get that. But we all stand to lose something here. And if we don't stop this, Amanda's going to become the mother of monsters."

"With all respect," says Tanis. "If she's the Internet, that's a bit late."

"Wait." Naree lays a hand on her partner's shoulder, worry luminous in her expression. "What do you mean 'mother of monsters'?"

"The creepypasta gods"—Cason rakes a hand through his hair—"are parasites. As far as I understand it. They're incubating inside Amanda, somehow. If they're not stopped, they're going to rip her apart."

"If you think I'm going to give a shit about what happened to the living incarnation of 4chan, you've got another thing—"

"*Tanis.*" But not even Naree's scandalised interjection is enough to diminish Tanis's ire.

The lines of Amanda's jaw draw tight and the light in her gaze goes flat. The smile that follows is functional, plastic, at odds with the blanched knuckles of her fists. She hesitates for a millisecond and then says, in an equally bland tone: "My personal connection to the problem isn't important. Just... You called me the living incarnation of 4chan. Think about what that implies." She starts blotting her fingers on the upholstery, as though trying to mop away something repulsive. "When we said the world would end, I think we may have misphrased it. The *world* won't end. It'd still be there. It'd just be under the stewardship of a new pantheon, worse than anything else you've seen.

The creepypasta gods are every dark impulse you've seen on social media, every word of hate, every cruel joke, every scrap of fear stirred up into rage. When humanity breathed faith into the old gods, it was to make sense of a world they feared, to make it safe. The new ones? They don't care. They *want* you afraid."

Amanda spreads her hands. "Is this the life you want for Beatrice?"

For a long time, no one speaks.

Tanis whispers throatily. "That's some cheesy fucking blackmail, you piece of shit. I—"

Whatever she's about to say goes unsaid. Beatrice, alerted by her name, wobbles out from the nursery, chubby arms held out for stability. I hadn't really taken time to inspect her in the car ride. At first look, she's all Naree: the same complexion, the same upturned nose, a smile that takes her whole face hostage. But when Tanis lopes after the girl, worry flashing across her expression, I can see where she takes after the other woman. They have the same eyes. And there's a precocious muscularity to Bee's motions that might make her a world-class athlete one day.

Or a hired gun, like her mother.

I staunch the impulse to ask if Tanis has watched *The Professional*. While I'm hardly known for my wisdom, even an idiot would know not to provoke *her*.

The light comes back to the universe, washes

outwards, spreads to wrap the little girl in gold. You could almost hear the Hallmark music gearing up. Bee swerves out of Tanis's encroaching embrace and totters defiantly up to the intruders in her home, boggling at us.

"I do not have candy and I regret being the only person here who has never handled a child," Fitz drawls.

I glance at him. "It's not just you. If it helps."

"I thought your ex had a kid?"

I pause. George was, *technically speaking*, a child. In many of the ways that mattered, he was also my step-child. As parent, I took my incumbency with the utmost seriousness. I filled the fridge flush with donations from the blood bank, the moistest cuts of meat. I made sure the doors were lamellared in talismans, kept every window locked, every vent obstructed by post-it wards. And I even let George drink my blood to encourage bonding.

But he wasn't at all a kid the way Beatrice is: cute, curious, and actually alive.

The fact that George had no skin and was, technically speaking, an eight-month-old fetus gouged from his mother's belly is completely tangential.

"It wasn't the same."

Fitz looks me over. "Mmm."

As Tanis scoops Bee into her embrace, Amanda

whispers, "Please. For your daughter. We cannot do this without you."

"Jesus fff—" She catches herself. "Fluffing cripes."

I nearly gnaw through my beer can, trying to waylay the impending laugh.

"I think that is as good an answer as you're going to get." Naree's shoulders loosen and she forces a hollow chuckle. "I think this is as good an answer as any of us will ever get. It's not about what we want. It's about what's good for Bee, right? Anyway. As long as they bring you back in one piece."

"We'll try," says Fitz, raking his eyes over Tanis's muscular frame. Thank Guan Yin there's nothing lecherous about his inspection; I get the feeling even the slightest indication of lust wouldn't go well. "But in the meantime," he continues, "there's one more mystery to solve."

"Please stop talking." Cason tents his hands over his mouth. "I don't even know what you're going to say, but just don't say it."

Of course, Fitz barrels past that.

"What's your special power?"

More silence before:

"She's a lamia," says Naree, brows arrowing.

"*Half*-lamia," Tanis adds. "Mother only had mortal men to breed with."

Something in her expression, the infinitesimal rise

of her smirk to a sneer, suggests that the story is more involved than that. But it couldn't have been anything good. Jouncing Bee in her embrace, she walks over to the television and sets the girl down. Some tinkering with the maze of electronics ensue before the theme song for *Teletubbies* begins blaring. Beatrice gurgles in obvious glee.

Cason tilts his head. "You're a snake creature?"

"Something like that."

"Okay. Uhm. What are lamias known for?" he continues.

"Super strength, incredible flexibility, Olympic-level athleticism." Naree begins counting nonchalantly off her fingers as she speaks. "Two dicks."

The room stops in its place save for the ambient noises of a deranged children's television program.

I can't tell who said the word first, but I don't think it matters. Within a second or so, we *all* say some variation of, "What?"

EIGHT

TANIS PALMS HER face, shoulders rustling.

Carson looks scandalized, and Fitz jams his knuckles into his mouth. Amanda is the only one of us not to move: stock-still, jaw slack, expression suspended in that tender place between amusement and horror. As a group, we are still recovering from that recent epiphany.

"*Naree.*" Tanis' voice is strangled.

"Nothing wrong about acknowledging the existence of good dick." Naree waggles her eyebrows.

"Especially when they come in a matching set."

"I feel like…" Amanda pauses, regroups, and tries again. "You know what? I feel like I lost the plot somewhere. Which isn't to say that this isn't *fascinating* data. Snakes have hemipenes. It stands to reason that a cryptid derived from reptilian stock would share such characteristics, but *seriously*. How does this relate to anything?"

The humour ebbs from Naree's expression. Lovingly, she reaches for Beatrice as the toddler waddles full-speed into the conversation, clutching the Teletubby she'd liberated from under a pyramid of folded laundry. Naree closes hands over the kid's ears and smiles sweetly up at us. Then, just there, a wobble in her voice: "Because you're stealing my wife away for a fucking suicide mission. The least I can do is make sure you die a little uncomfortable."

"If you've changed your mind about this, I'll remind you that I wasn't onboard with this at all." Tanis takes Bee's hand and shepherds her back to the television.

Carson rises, moves to collect the cans we've emptied and scattered across the living room, his gait stilt-legged, awkward: a puppet's disjointed walk. "Sorry, we're making a hell of a mess."

"That's fine," says Naree dismissively. "Just leave it."

"We're being terrible guests."

"Really. It's fine."

"I just want to help—"

"Put the clutter down or I shoot you in the head," Tanis snarls.

A sweet voice exults: "Shoot!"

"Look at what you did." Tanis stops herself short of a rude gesture and swings down as Bee comes barrelling away from her programme yet again, clearly having decided that this was the most productive way of accruing attention. The exasperation in Tanis's expression, worn smooth by constant use, suggests she's aware of the manipulation. "Come on, honey. The adults are talking. Do you want *Dora the Explorer* instead?"

"Shoot you!" Bee repeats.

Tanis hoists her up. "That's not a nice thing to say."

"Shoot you... please?"

"I guess that's an improvement," says Tanis.

"Anyway," continues Naree. "It's no big deal. You should still stay the course. This matters. All of it still matters. Amanda made it clear. I get why this needs to happen and why Tanis needs to go with you. But that doesn't change the fact she's the love of my life and there's a part of my head that says she's not coming back. I don't know what I'm supposed to do if I'm right. So, I'm going to be petty. Just a little bit. Just for a moment. And that's all that is.." She taps her breastbone with a finger. Bee, picking up, maybe, on the fact that her mothers are in distress, twists in Tanis's embrace. Her breath begins to hitch, the thin beginnings of a wail expanding in her throat.

Tanis, rocking Bee in her arms: "Babe, is that really everything?"

I clear my throat. "Should we give you guys some privacy?"

"*Shut up*," the two women snap in unison.

Fitz gives me a sympathetic shrug and slinks towards their fridge, carefully extracting the remnants of our six-pack of artisanal beer and holding it up. Amanda demurrs and Carson flatly ignores him, so he comes around the tableau and sinks onto the moss-green couch beside me.

I crack open a beer, earning another glare.

"Naree," Tanis tries again, when the sound of my beer's enthusiastic foaming ebbs away. "Babe—"

"This is hard, okay? Being complicit in all of this. Telling you to go. Telling you to put yourself at risk. Telling you it's okay to, maybe, die for a bigger purpose when all I want is for you to stay home, stay here, stay with me and be safe and I..."

"I thought I made it clear. I was outright askin' you for—ssh, Bee, just give me a second—your opinion. If you don't want me to go, I won't. I swear to god—"

"If I had said something, you'd have just thrown everyone out!"

"That's my point!"

"No. No, it isn't! Not my point, at least. My feelings don't matter here. We don't even need to have this discussion. I just... I just needed to let off some steam, okay? Just a little bit. Can we please stop discussing this?"

"No. This actually sounds like it's important to you."

"You are making a big deal out of—"

"Probably not."

"See?"

"I feel like someone should be steering this conversation away from this route," I say.

Tanis doesn't even look over. "Shut up."

"Shutting up again," I say. "Man, I feel like I've been saying that a lot—"

"*Shut*—"

"Got it."

Naree collects the toddler into her arms, head downturned. "I love you. I love the fact you'd give up everything for me, risk everything for me. Which is why we're doing this. You need to go save the world. Because if you don't, there's not going to be a future for Bee. We owe it to her to be strong."

"I'm coming back."

Naree shrugs a shoulder, face still obscured by the waterfall of her hair, but her voice is steady. "If you don't come back, I'm going to find you. I'm going straight down to Hell and I'm going to find you, and I'm going to drag you back, and I'm going to beat you with a shoe."

"You sound like your mother."

Naree laughs, shrill and loud and long, and it cuts through the fraying tendon of Beatrice's certainty that the world is alright. Her eyes go round and then her mouth follows, her face concaving into the howl that follows.

"Aw, heck. Bee. I'm sorry. Sssh. Amma didn't mean—Ssh, ssh. It'll be okay." There's a sheen of tears on her cheeks. She holds Bee close, bouncing the child at a jagged tempo until she finds one that blunts her daughter's howling. She vanishes into the nursery, and the door is mule-kicked shut behind her.

Another silence tightens around the room.

"I hate all of you," Tanis announces after a full five minutes.

"We don't have to like each other to save the world," says Amanda.

"If it's any consolation," Cason joins in. "*We* don't like each other very much."

I snort. "Hey, speak for yourself. I like you guys just fine. It's *myself* I hate."

Tanis stalks through the room, stopping by a liquor cabinet; she wrenches the doors open and pries out a glossy-looking bottle of bourbon. The cork is popped, and Tanis downs a quick swallow and wipes her mouth on the back of her hand. "You know what pisses me off the most? The fact that you're springing this on me now. Naree and I never even got the chance to be married! We were just—"

"I could fix that," says Amanda.

"What are you talking—?" Tanis's eyes go wide; her irises shift from brown to serpentine yellow, almost to gold. "You could?"

"It wouldn't take very much," the clone continues modestly. "It's just a question of records. But if you want a ceremony, I... I don't know if I'd be the best person to ask for something like that. If you don't mind the informality—"

"You know, *I* could help with that part of the equation."

"What—forget it." Tanis looks at me, puzzled. "Alright, Einstein. What's your deal?"

"I'm going to ignore the fact that sounded like an insult. Um, it wouldn't be legal in the eyes of America, but I guess that Amanda is taking care of that part of it."

"It's been a long, long day. Cut to the chase."

"Well, in theory, I'm probably—I'm at least as

good as any priest you'd find. Most clergymen tend to not actually be *personally* anointed by their, uhm, employers, if you know what I mean? If you don't mind the fact that I was consecrated by Hell rather than Heaven, and—"

"Again, it's been a long day. Keep it moving." ."

"Let me officiate your wedding. I'm about as close to an—and I can't believe I'm saying this—authentic holy man as we're going to get on short notice. Amanda can make the official part of things happen. I can do the ceremony. We can get you married. It's not ideal, but it's something, and if the worst happens, at least..." My voice drains away. "You know."

Tanis considers it for a moment. "Well, I guess Naree isn't religious, and well, I don't know what I am." She takes another slug of the bourbon, her expression raw, halfway to hope, halfway to despair. But there is a new brightness there. "This sounds either like the worst idea in the world, or something Naree and I are going to laugh over in thirty years. Assuming we survive that long. So, you know what? Let's do this. I'm going to wait until Naree is done in the shower and I'll see about proposing."

Amanda clears her throat. "If you don't already have a ring, there are two hundred and forty-five prospective sellers within driving distance. Apparently, Orlando's not the happiest place in the world for marriages."

*　　*　　*

AND THAT, ANG moh, is how I got into the wedding business.

NINE

READER, I MARRY them.

It is not the ceremony that anyone might have coveted, bereft of grandeur. There are no bands, no musicians in three-hundred dollar tuxedos, satin around their waists and a smile on their faces. There is no champagne, only cheap beer procured in bulk from the ramshackle gas station three blocks down. No gazebo, no fairy lights strung in the willow trees, no cake so elaborate you'd feel guilty for even desecrating it with a breath. Nothing of those components essential to a fairytale wedding.

Instead, they have us.

They have Bee.

And most importantly, they have each other.

We come by the next day, after several excursions to some of Orlando's many fried chicken venues. None of which, let me tell you, come within spitting distance of Malaysia's ayam goreng, with its myriad of spices, its fish sauce marinade. The Americans, of course, pooh-pooh it as nationalism, but I know who wins the fast food wars.

Spoiler: it isn't the people who invented it.

But that is a collateral fun fact. What matters is that I marry Naree and Tanis by the dwindling wolf-light, the firmament burnt indigo by the encroaching night. Dusk this evening is bands of gold and rose, the horizon flushed with phoenix colours.

"I think I'm going to cry," Fitz whispers to me while we stand under the first stars, waiting for Naree to walk down the dew-spangled grass to where Tanis waits for her. Earlier today, we cleared their backyard of Bee's little yellow-pink push-car, and moved the rest of the mess—garden rakes, stray cigarette butts, a graveyard of nicotine patches, a few cans of energy drinks—into a plastic castle, the face of a luridly grinning princess emblazoned forever on one tower.

"Me too." I worry at the little bow-tie I'm wearing. "You clean up okay."

He mocks a bow. "Why thank you, sir."

"I have to ask," Cason says, coming over. "When was the last time you actually put on—" He flicks me on the underside of my chin and I straighten, startled. The distraction is apparently what he's angling for as he lunges for my bow-tie. "*Jesus*, stop moving. You're squirming like a kid at prom." He achieves whatever he's hoping for and straightens with a sigh. "How's that?"

"It's a bit tight."

"How did you survive getting so old?" Cason might be the oldest guy in the room, but the way he rolls his eyes at me, you'd think he was fifteen and damned by hippie parents.

"We really have to sit down one day and discuss what 'survive' means in my neck of the woods. It's not as clear-cut as you think."

No such thing as *perfect* in a world worn down by gods and worse. Three Stooges gone to seed, a woman who is the entire digital world, a picnic spread of whatever we could forage in the gas station. You could ask for a lot more for a wedding. But we're trying, and hopefully this will be close enough. If nothing else, we have fairy lights.

Tanis comes out of the house first: still muscular,

still don't-fuck-with-me, but so much more elegant in a subtle pinstripe suit with heels I'd assumed she wouldn't be seen dead in. The trousers are high-waisted, held up by braces. The black vest might as well be painted on. Tanis holds the jacket hooked on a finger and over her shoulder. Every curl gleams, lacquered into place, luminous as the smile she wears so nervously.

"How'd I look?"

"Like your father would die proud," I whisper.

She winces. "Yeah, I have no idea about that. He'd certainly be *surprised*."

Her gaze drifts. Cason throws the last coil of fairy lights into the trees and steps back, fists on his hips, a satisfied nod coming to fruit once he realizes for sure that the foliage won't catch fire. He looks back to us and salutes with a double thumbs-up before scurrying back into the house. Piano music drifts out, slow and breathless, slightly plinky, but hey, we're making do.

Then Naree steps out.

And she is glorious.

I don't know how, but by some trick of nature, the sunset sinks into Naree's thick black hair. It gilds her skin. It turns the sequins of her dress into an inferno: orange-gold melting into the deepest plum. Her shoulders are bare, her throat collared by a circlet in the form of a snake. It is her only decoration; the only one she needs. I breathe out, slowly.

"You know," Tanis whispers, voice harsh with emotion, as Naree pads barefooted towards us, hand-in-hand with Bee, who is dressed like an angel complete with a fuzzy golden halo (the fact it resembles a toilet brush tarted up with tinsel is irrelevant to the moment). "You know, I never thought this was going to be my life. If the price for this happiness is living through everything I did, I'd do it again. I'd do it ten times. I'll do anything for them."

"I think—" I clear my throat. Fitz sidles to an appropriate distance, the rings in the cup of his palm. "That the feeling is mutual. I get the feeling that Naree would go through Hell for you."

"Fuck *that*," Tanis glances over her shoulder, a wry smile crooked like a gun with its safety off. "My girl would take over Hell and have us lord over it as queen and queen, assuming anyone was stupid enough to even think up a stunt like that. I mean, look at her. Who'd risk *her* wrath?"

"What are we talking about?" Naree grins as she draws into earshot, Bee migrated into her arms. If the bittersweetness of the situation appals me at all, Naree shows no sign of it. "Is this more end-of-the-world crap? How amazing I look? It's about how amazing I look, isn't it?

"A little of column A, a little of column B." I manage a lean smile. "I'm sorry I couldn't get you a priest."

"Pfff." Naree straight-up cackles, her glee bright as as the love on her face, her fingers coming to twine with Tanis's own. The lamia kisses her knuckles, a courtly gesture. "Like we could have gotten a Catholic priest who does gay weddings on short notice."

"Amanda could have found you one." Fitz nods towards the avatar, standing in a garbage-bag-bloom of a baby-blue bridesmaid dress. The expression on her face has suffered its way into a kind of worn-down repose. I don't know which of the two mandated this outfit, and I am not going to ask.

"Eh. Doesn't matter." A flutter of Naree's gloved fingers. "Not like I believe in that crap, anyway."

"I'm still struggling to see how you're holding onto your atheism in this epoch of bonafide killer gods," I mumble.

Tanis offers me an arctic look. "No one asked you."

"Fair enough." Coughing into a fist, I let my attention veer away, and take in the sight. One day, someone will ask what the dimensions of happiness are. I'll tell them it is the width of a home and the span of two lovers' smiles. "Ladies and gentlemen—"

"*Ladies*, he says." Naree giggles into her palms. "You clearly haven't seen how Tanis eats—"

"Ssh," Tanis says.

"Love you too."

"*Anyway*. We are gathered here today to see these two wonderful people united in"—I pause—"unholy matrimony, I guess. Technically, because of my infernal associations and the lack of nuance in Western culture, I'm—"

A grossly dissonant clatter of chords. Cason bellows from indoors: "Get on with it! And could you speak up?"

"Sorry!" I yell back before clearing my throat with even more purpose. Bee smushes a tiny hand into my nose, ecstatic at the opportunity for mischief. "If anyone has any objections, I'm sure that Tanis will, quite literally, tear them from your tongue."

"Damn straight."

"So, let's skip along past the parts I don't really have a clue about and get on with it. Do you, Tanis, last name unknown because that's how we roll, take Naree, last name also unknown because the end times don't give much room for formalities, as your lawfully wedded wife for so long as you two may live—"

"Longer. I'll love you longer than that."

"That wasn't the question."

Tanis ignores me. She laces one hand with Naree's, the other she raises for Bee's inspection. After some deliberation, the little girl presses her hand onto her mother's raised palm. When Tanis speaks again, her voice is throaty: "Even after there is no more Earth to walk and Tartarus has gone to dust and there is nothing but the void, I'll still love you. I'll still call you my wife. You are my everything, Naree. Since the day I first met you, you've been a light in my life. No matter where the future takes me, I'll follow your light home. I promise you. I love you. I will always, always love you."

"I love you too." The words come so softly from Naree's lips, I almost do not hear.

I look between them, swallowing. I wonder about the history there. You can see it in the way they hold hands: not like new lovers, no, not like people who'd never lost nights to the idea that one day this person would be gone, leaving them alone in a bed suddenly colder than they remembered. When I trust myself to speak again, I continue, voice husked of what little gravitas it ever had. "Do you, Naree—"

"Don't worry, I got this." Again, that radiant smile. Maudlin reactions aside, I'm beginning to feel slightly extraneous to the proceedings. But that's okay. This isn't about me. "Tanis Barlas. From the moment we started talking online, I knew you were going to be the one, that this was it, that you were going to be my one and only for so long as we live. Did you know I have nightmares about the what-ifs? What if we'd never met? What if you'd caught me on a bad day and decided you couldn't care for someone like me?"

"That wouldn't have happened." Tanis half-stumbles over the words in her hurry to get them out.

"Ssh. It's my turn to monologue." Naree straightens. "I don't believe in souls, or eternity, or an afterlife, or any of that crap. My faith in those things is currently in review. But I know I love you, and I will want you as my wife so long as even an atom of me still exists in the universe. They say that our reality is nothing but a simulation, so I'm kinda feeling optimistic. I'm going to figure out how this works and I will make us last forever while you go save the world."

"Naree…"

"So, you gotta come back. You better fucking come back."

To everyone's astonishment, or at least *mine*, it is Amanda who speaks up first: "If we have to buy her passage home with our lives, we will."

"Would it completely wreck the moment if I took this opportunity to point out that you, at least in context of this particular body, are a clone and there's a million of you waiting in a vat somewhere?"

"Only seventy-five."

"Well, that's egg on *my* face." I raise a hand and count to ten. "But it's not like I've got anything to really live for anymore. Dying to make sure two lovers come back together doesn't seem like a bad idea. I'm in."

Fitz crooks a wan smile. "For Bee."

"For Bee," the rest of us echo.

TEN

CHEAP BOOZE IS like drunken anonymous sex: excellent in theory, hollow in implementation. The gas station beer doesn't last long in the polls, not with the memory of Naree's chocolate stout still coating the back of our throats. We try to get Tanis to part with her bourbon, but even the endorphin-rush of impromptu matrimony isn't enough to convince her. Which, as kids today might phrase it, *sucks*.

But no one pushes too hard. It's a wedding; decisions are the prerogative of the brides squared. We drain our inventory of low-price alcohol, make two and a half trips back to the gas station to restock. The third jaunt is my fault, aborted because I felt a fell compulsion to provide the wedding party with something other than cheese and crackers.

"Cheese beer soup," I slur happily.

Cason sits up from the couch. "I'm game."

"With bacon," I continue.

"No one's arguing, Rupert." Fitz flails an arm at the room. Tanis glances over, an eyebrow cranked up to her hairline. She perches on the lip of a windowsill, Naree clamped between her thighs, one arm in the small of her new wife's back.

"Beer. Soup," she deadpans.

Naree smacks her. "Like you wouldn't eat the pot yourself."

A shrug follows. No longer irradiated with menace, Tanis has become an easier person to study. The reptilian element is less overt than I'd have thought, manifested primarily in the way light sometimes pools in her eyes and that liquid, loose-boned grace.

"He calls himself a chef," she retorts, a challenge drowsing in her smirk. "He should be able to come up with something better—"

"*Hey*," I say. "Hey. Excuse me. It's not my fault your kitchen's a wreck."

"Easy." Smiling, Naree wags a finger at me,

pirouetting away from Tanis, who reaches out a second too late, fingers grazing the hem of Naree's tasselled dress. "It's our house you're takin' shots at."

I crowbar myself out of the armrest and stagger towards the kitchen island, counting each step, one after another in single file. I'm a five-foot-eight man with a criminal history. I don't think I'm legally *allowed* to be a lightweight. Outside, the sky looks washed-out, the black soaked through with orange-blue light pollution. Like home, I decide, hiraeth a needle scratched over glass, leaving a fine crack in my mood. But like any kind of damage, it can be remedied with a strategically placed cover.

"I'm not taking shots at you," I howl, louder than needed, louder than longing for a country that wouldn't think twice about revoking my citizenship. It's probably fortunate that Amanda has command of the kidlet in the makeshift nursery, or there wouldn't even be this pastiche of a wedding party. "But I might be taking offense at the fact you haven't gone grocery shopping in ever."

"There's kimchi." Naree pouts.

"Kimchi does not a pantry make."

That brings her up short. She breathes in, lets it go in a brisk huff. "Also, there's gochujang paste."

"Again, that's not enough—you know what? I'm just going to check the fridge one more time. Maybe you have lap cheong. And eggs. I could do something with lap cheong and eggs, a bit of sweet potato, some bacon. You're American."

"I ..." A beat and breath wisps past, before Naree adds in laughing tones, "I would be offended if I didn't actually love bacon. So. Carry on."

Triumphant, I swing open the refrigerator door. Earlier reconnaissance had divulged—well, not nothing, but a surfeit of below-average ingredients. Withered mushrooms; tofu past its sell-date; rotisserie chicken, delicately nibbled; a riveting display of baby foods, contained within individual jars, some home-made, some not; barbeque sauces; a single cucumber mysteriously haloed in the misty light of the bulb.

Then something blinks.

Eyes in the back wall of the refrigerator. Human, entirely so. Down to the sockets sunken into the white plastic, the lacing of capillaries, as though of someone who'd not slept well for days. Blue eyes, blanched pale as frost. I jerk away, tripping with a loud yelp. The others come staggering over as I backpedal, the door swinging half-shut. My heart is in my throat.

"What the fuck?"

It takes thirty seconds to realize I hadn't been the one to say it.

"Eyes," I babble. "You had eyes in your fridge. Also, thank Guan Yin. I thought it was the fridge talking."

Naree looms into view. "Okay, your jokes are starting to get just a little bit—"

"No, no. Like. Actual eyes, in the back of your fridge."

"Are you drunk?"

I look in Fitz's direction. He isn't wrong, per se: I *am* drunk. Ignominiously so, in fact. But hardly drunk enough to *hallucinate*. "You really asking me that?"

Even inebriated, Tanis is preternaturally quiet. She sinks to a crouch beside me, staring into the cold light from inside the fridge. The stillness of her itches at my hindbrain.

"What did you see?" she asks.

"A pair of blue eyes in the back of the fridge."

"Rolling around on a shelf?"

"No. Embedded in the back wall." I unfold from the floor, dusting myself off. "You guys wouldn't happen to be having a demon infestation, would you?"

"Could it be those—" Cason has changed since we began our debauchery. The softness is gone: he's still about forty pounds above optimal, stomach cambering fractionally over his belt, but now there's something different. A tautening of his stance: shoulders back, arms ready, an aura of anticipation, his gait light. Boxer, I decide. Before he made the epiphanous change to 'dad.' "You know."

"If it is, it isn't very good at hiding." Tanis grinds

through clenched teeth, voice low, peculiarly soporific, quietly predatory in a way that hints at the moment before the lunge, the strike, the kill. "Which is useful."

"Rupert might just be seeing things," Fitz quips, lofting himself onto the kitchen island.

"Not sure if you parsed it the first time, but I feel like it is amazingly hypocritical for a prophet—"

"Chronicler."

"—whatever, to have the temerity to question my grip on sanity, when you routinely get assaulted by ambient, *buh*, radio signals."

"Hey. It's a profession."

"You're a malfunctioning satellite dish. Shut up. Also, what were we talking about?"

Cason's voice floats over, even-keeled. "Amanda might have an idea."

Tanis, ever pragmatic, spares no time for our nonsense. She tiptoes over to the fridge, curls a finger around the door and waves Naree back. Her wife complies with easy fluidity, although not before taking possession of a cast-iron frying pan.

Tanis nods once to us before swinging the door open hard enough to slam it into the wall, cracking the dry plaster. We jump as one, swearing in a scatter of languages. Cason vaults over the island, Fitz goes the other way. Naree, despite initial expectations, torpedoes towards the appliance, pan over her head.

But there's nothing.

Condensation whorls out of the refrigerator, lapping at the sepia tiles. The single cucumber glows in the luminance. We stand there in puzzled communion with the gods of wait-what-happened, before Tanis breaks the silence with a faint, "Huh."

Naree lowers her weaponry, equally flummoxed, and picks her way over. "That was a bit… anticlimactic."

"Well, I'm sorry nothing jumped out to kill us."

Tanis, however, does not relax. Her silhouette remains framed in the white glow, every muscle still taut. "Huuuh," she says again, dragging the sound out. When she does deign to withdraw a step, even that comes across as a move to allow more room to manoeuvre. Tanis paces like a trapped carnivore. Now and again, she repeats herself, whispering, "Huh."

Fitz takes first swing at the silence. "If you say 'huh' one more—"

"There's something there."

We freeze.

"Like, a cucumber?" I manage.

The lamia glares balefully at me but says nothing, features pinched and pensive. She swings the door of the refrigerator shut and opens it again, only to slam it closed for a second time. The ritual repeats itself several times over, abrading everyone's nerves, before at last Cason, of all people, cracks.

"What *is* it?" He leans over the kitchen counter, both palms on the formica, and tries in vain to peer behind the offending appliance.

"I don't *know*," says Tanis. "That's the problem. But I know it's there."

"That isn't very helpful," I note, helpfully.

Another glare.

"Whatever that thing is, it doesn't seem particularly smart. I can still smell it." Her tongue dips out of her mouth, just for a half-second, *tasting*. "It's here, and it thinks it can hide in plain sight? Or at least, that's what it feels like. Something less stupid would have squirmed away to regroup."

Cason palms a shoulder and begins rolling the joint on its axis, back and forth, back and forth, a boxer testing his flexibility. "So, let's kill it."

"I see *someone's* channelling his grandfather."

"Yes." His face is impassive. "If that's what will keep Bee safe. In case you've forgotten, there's a child in the next room…"

"I don't know about Fitz or Rupert, but *we* haven't." Naree returns her frying pan to its hook and leans a hip against the kitchen island, Tanis still walking angry circuits in front of the fridge. "I also don't think this banter is going to help. Let's discuss what we know. First, it *exists*. Second, it seems to be interested in someone in the room. Third, no one else has seen it and we've all been here since like seven. No one except for Rupert. Now, how is Rupert different from anyone—?"

"Oh, fuck me. If there's another possessed crocodile god coming to eat me, I swear I'm just going to jump into the oven which, by the way, is *a very nice oven*—"

My left-field flattery knocks Naree askew. "Uh. Thank you?"

"—and, you know, just start basting myself with garlic butter until my thigh melts off the bone. How about that?"

"Is it normal that I'm actually starting to get hungry?"

No one humours Fitz with acknowledgment. Tanis, who'd stood with her head cocked throughout Naree's analysis, nods once to herself and closes the distance between us. She claps both hands on my shoulders, a very fraternal gesture; the friendliest she'd ever been. And I might, perhaps, have relished the olive branch if it hadn't come with Tanis's fingers biting into my flesh.

"Ow," I inform her, hopefully.

"Rupert," Tanis says, paying no attention at all to my discomfort. "I need you to listen to me. If Naree is right, and I trust Naree to be right—"

"Thanks, babe!"

"—you're going to need to keep this together. If you

start panicking, you're going to put everyone else at risk. We're right here with you. You're not alone. We need you to keep calm so we can figure this out."

"What's option B?"

"There's no option B. If you don't cooperate, I'm going to break both your arms and both your legs." Her smile is frayed but sincere, completely divorced from the threat.

"Dictatorial rule. I can get behind that." I suppose it is grim testimony to the toxic patterns of my life that I find being strong-armed peculiarly reassuring. I blame the ghouls. You always know where you stand with someone who will threaten dismemberment and mean it. There's none of the idioms, the what-ifs, the did-they-mean-what-I-think-what-they-meants. And in this overly complicated world, I like it. "Okay. So, what do you want me to do?"

Another exchange of portentous looks, then Naree declares, quite gaily, "It's a wedding. Let's go get some BBQ."

ELEVEN

I FUCKING LOVE Korean barbeque. I love gogi gui so much that it actually succeeds in anaesthetising my terror, leaving me drunk, ravenous, and happy to die so long as someone keeps spooning me rich mouthfuls of jumulleok right to the end. The restaurant that Naree picks out is, to no one's surprise, the real deal: a hole-in-the-wall extravaganza packed to the lungs with people. The perfume of sizzling meat shimmers through the air. I can smell galbi of every kind. Were I not almost entirely certain that this is a bad idea and we are all going to suffer grievous bodily harm, I'd think I was in heaven.

"Who wants soju?" asks Naree.

A round of hands shoot up.

"Anyone here lactose-intolerant?" she continues.

Cason tilts his head, confused. "Are you ordering eggnog?"

"Not a terrible idea, but I don't think we're close enough to Christmas. No, the first round is going to be makgeolli."

"Geseunheit," Fitz says.

"Do *not* make racist jokes at my wedding—"

"That wasn't where I was going with that!" He throws his arms up, almost broadsiding an Asian woman of indeterminable age. I'd hazard her to be in her late thirties, early forties, but I'd rather have my intestines strung across the interstate than ask. She collects herself and smiles thinly at Fitz, an expression that might be parsed as friendly, but only if you're blind. Under her withering stare, Fitz shrinks, mouthing sorries until she steps around him to pad over to Naree.

Her eyes make an orbit of our table, expression shifting between subtle disapproval and even subtler disappointment. Naree alone, it seems, merits warmth. The two have a short exchange in Korean before she prowls away.

"Alright. Yoghurty rice wine coming our way." Naree claps her hands together. Tanis has shed her wedding attire for a more practical get-up: leather jacket, undershirt, boots, blue jeans strung with chains. Naree, on the other hand, has not. She practically glows in the restaurant's oddly harsh lighting, dark hair crowned by a single purple orchid. "Now we get to the fun part. How many of you have gone to a Korean BBQ?"

Cason and I raise our hands.

"How many of you can cook?"

"Define 'cook,'" says Fitz.

"Bacon, french toast, scrambled eggs—does that count?" says Cason.

"Depends on how well they're received."

"My kids have not died of food poisoning yet."

"Have you ever gotten a *compliment* for your cooking?" Naree folds her arms under her breasts and leans forward, which has the three of us scrabbling to look in every direction but cleavage. The giggle that follows is not malevolent, per se, but it has certainly considered malevolence.

"I have been told it's wonderfully serviceable by the wife," Cason replied.

I look over at him. "That isn't a compliment."

"My wife has exacting standards."

"Being told that you are competent at mediocrity is *not* a compliment."

Naree interrupts. "Bride calls vetoing power. No more jabbering. Rupert, stop poking fun at the soccer dad. Settle this outside."

"I would, but I don't want to get eaten by a crocodile." Pause for effect. "Again."

"Then *behave*." She kills the conversation for a full minute. Naree is at least five years younger than the rest of us, but bears the authority of a dowager. It is ancient and indomitable, the spirit of every auntie to have ever lived distilled into a single incandescent glare. As someone repeatedly broken over the knee of destiny, and an Asian man raised in a traditional household, I'm not unfamiliar with the look. There's something unsettling about wanting to squeak, 'Yes, Mom' to a woman who, from certain angles, reminds me of a child's doll.

The server comes back, giving Fitz a wide berth and narrowed eyes. Alcohol is distributed across the table to a chorus of gratified noises. Only when the clamour has died down and we've each received our share does the server, tray at a rakish angle, start inquiring about meat.

The short answer is: we order everything. Loudly, with lurid enthusiasm, stumbling over each other's requests, Cason trying and failing to referee, while the rest of us shout and stomp. Our waitress receives the chatter without expression, her face still haunted by the echo of that thin-lipped smile.

From the outside, I imagine we probably look like drunks gone wild. But really, we're here because gods don't like witnesses. Demons neither. Nothing that has ever been pinned to a page in mythology cares for unsolicited scrutiny, and it's all because of faith. Humanity reprogrammed itself to always gravitate towards the factual, the real, the truth, as determined by a billions-strong jury of its peers. In the face of wonder, our species now says, 'Wait. Where's the hidden camera?'

And that, in turn—or so Amanda assured us as she warbled *Watership Down* to Bee—is nothing less than a two-ton sledgehammer blow to a body already asphyxiating on the sermons of a thousand celebrity atheists. Without a proper framework, the divine and the dastardly are nothing but mist to be burnt away by an incredulous sun. So that's why we're here: if anything is tailing me, hoping to make loh mien out of my intestines, it would need to be subtle.

Also, we're starving.

Mostly that, actually.

The woman leaves and then she comes back with galbi in various styles and marinades, king mushrooms cut thin for the grill, bulgogi steaming in a stone bowl, fish in garlic butter, pork belly red with spices, as much bak chan as she can jigsaw onto our table, and vegetables that no one touches. Naree takes charge of the grilling process, delegating the distribution to Cason, and alcohol duty to Tanis, who tops up everyone's glass with an expression that softens, over the course of two glasses, from brooding to bemusedly at ease.

"You know, we can't hide here forever," Fitz observes.

I bring my bowl of rice up to my face, spear an unattended lobe of pickled garlic and shovel a mouthful of carbohydrates and onion-crowned bulgogi into my face before I speak. "You sure? I mean, if we spoke to the management, told them that two out of five can cook, we might be able to come to a bed-and-breakfast-and-total-servitude arrangement."

Naree drops sweet potato rounds onto the grill. "We have a daughter."

"It'd be culturally appropriate for her to—no? Okay. Let the record show that I apologized and gave up the tasteless joke right there. Sorry. Seriously. No need to punch me."

"You don't always *need*"—Tanis takes care to stretch out the syllable, smiling coldly—"to punch someone. Sometimes, you just *want* to."

"But you know, Fitz's got a point." Naree juts her chin at the Chronicler. The crowd is beginning to thin. No one has yet made any hints about us leaving, but it is probably imminent. "We can't hide here forever. Someone's got to figure out what the fuck is stalking you."

"Not me,' said Tanis. 'Can't smell *shit* here."

I look between everyone and down at the grill, the cast-iron still smouldering with the odiferous apparitions of cooked meats past. I stare at the shreds of skin cooked onto the metal, the fat charred black, and I sigh, the sound of a man who hadn't just given up but is resigned to tying his own noose. "What do you guys know about black magic?"

"It's not a great way to impress an angel on a date?" says Fitz.

Tanis curls her lip; when she speaks, there's a newly sibilant quality to her voice. "My mother, I suppose, was divinely gifted, but her magic was as black as sludge, if you ask me. What do I know about it? It *takes*. It corrupts. It always makes you pay more than it is worth. That's what I know."

I nod, adrenaline frissoning through my limbs. Through the alcohol haze, it feels like the hand of a grandfather clock metronoming in my skull, cushioned by cotton. I shiver and swallow, willing down the twitching energy. I feel like a meth-head on a three-day bender, my heart clattering against my ribs. I know what I have to do next, and I don't like it.

"Yeah. No. Yes. Kind of. That isn't wrong." I seesaw a hand, while the others watch me like a man tightrope-walking across the lip of a rooftop. "It's about pain. Yours, someone else's. Something has to hurt. The exchange is always about pain. But in an impersonal kind of way, you know? No one's actually out to cause malice for the fun of it. Not usually. It's really quite civil."

I take a shuddering breath.

"I really should stop babbling and get this show on the road, you know?"

Before anyone can stop me, I bring my palm down on the grill and pour the sum of my focus into not screaming as my hand sizzles to a sweet-smelling crisp.

THE WORLD SNAPS, pops, erupts like a blown bulb as the pain climbs to a pitch that I've still yet to find words for. Slowly, I chant through chattering teeth, my uninjured hand squeezing the wrist of the hand that's still cooking, cooking down to the bone. This was easier when I had Bob, and Bill, and Andy, and all the dime-store demons who used to rent squares of my skin. But we make do.

Reality clarifies to a neon blue overlaid with moving shapes, so bright that the colour sears my eyes. I think someone is screaming for me to stop, to move my hand, but they might as well be trying to lasso an iceberg for all the good it's doing. And my skin is beginning to blacken, and I wonder how long before I hit bone. I press down harder and magic swirls deliriously through my vision.

Black for humans, for things safe and simple. Whitish-pink like exposed muscle for everything else, shining from the hemispheres of Fitz's brain, from Cason's every pore, from the coil of Tanis's spine. "Nothing. It's not here. Piece of shit was probably just a domovoi playin' with us," I mumble, wondering already if Diyu would mind too much if I stabbed myself in the lungs for a get-out-of-hideous-disfigurement card.

"Okay, can someone shoot—?"

The words peel away.

"Fuck," I whisper. "It's on the ceiling."

I raise the singed lump that was my hand towards the ceiling, a finger pointed straight up at the horror weaving sinuously along the beams. Amniotic ooze drips in gleaming strings from toothed limbs, as many as necessary to invoke trouser-staining terror. No one else notices, or seems to care. It swivels nearly one-eighty to gaze full upon me, grinning. Somewhere in the genetic makeup, there had been a cat—you can see it in the arrowing of its ears, the contours of its skull—but the resemblance is vestigial.

Its mouth bleeds where it has been coerced too far from its natural shape, become a fretwork of bloodied nodules. Eyes open diagonally along its brows; its face is honeycombed by them, like a lotus root bulbous with unnatural fruit. It gets worse from there. The attenuated spiral of limbs, bunched together like a ribcage cracked slightly open. The twist of organs. The *smell*.

Guan Yin, the smell.

Holding eye contact, it lowers itself behind the back of Naree's head. Slowly, so slowly I can count the attoseconds between each passing moment, it unhinges its jaw. Static shimmers across the gunk-sticky mess of its pelt, like a ripple of poisoned silver.

Somewhere nearby, I can hear someone whispering, a sermon like the howl of desert winds, like the thundering of war bands and the percussions of their feet; like the musk of a leopard, its shadow stretched long over the sand; like a woman's wine-weathered laugh, low and growling.

"Sekhmet," says Fitz's voice, clear as a bell.

She smiles at the mention of her name and her eyes bleed black. Sekhmet tilts herself forward, while I sit, suspended in my horror, pain roiling in waves. Naree's head fits perfectly within that cavernous maw, the dentition layered as a lamprey's. A scream builds in the house of my lungs, but already it's too late.

Then Naree jackknifes forward, away and out of reach, snarling, "Fuck. That."

And just like that, in the immortal words of Ice Cube, it's on like *Donkey Kong*.

Cue battle music.

TWELVE

WHAT HAPPENS FIRST is that Naree picks up the earthenware bowl that had until recently sat mountainous with bibimbap and cudgels an Egyptian goddess. *Twonk*. Sekhmet howls like a cat hosed down with hot grease.

"—the fuck is that thing?" Cason, snarling. Coming out of my fugue is like having my head wrenched out of a bowl of molasses: a sucking sensation like my ears are being flushed, before clarity returns, along with colour, speech, the pain as the air hits a hand scorched clean of living nerves. I suck in a breath, hissing.

Fingers knot in the fabric of my shirt and haul me backwards out of my seat, nearly causing me more injuries as the chair tips over and I tumble out. But Cason, for all his apparent softness, moves me like a sack of potatoes, effortlessly and with only minimal compassion.

Fitz is still standing slack-jawed, intoning prophecies and psalms to the glories of the mutated horror hissing at us all. His eyes suppurate ink. "All hail thee, goddess, Dread Lioness of Khem, She Who Must Be Obeyed, the All-Conquering Queen. We love you with the blood of our bodies and the blood of our enemies; we feast in your name, we conquer for your—"

"Why the fuck haven't you two started doing anything *useful?*" Surprising no one, least of all me, Tanis is the only one with a gun out, firing at point-blank range into the warped skull. The bullets do nothing. Sekhmet grins at her, giddy, her attention seduced by a new toy. Tanis dodges the goddess's first playful swipe with ease but by the third, the fourth attempt, I can see sweat glossing her tanned skin and hear her panting like a sled dog.

"Someone fucking do something useful," Tanis shouts again.

Naree volunteers. "I could hit her with the bowl again?"

"That was surprisingly effective." I wobble into something approximating an upright position. The pain is less transcendent now: no longer holy but no less powerful, still a throbbing supernova of Jesus-fuck anguish, like a fever, like necrosis at double speed, rotting away all awareness of the world save for that agony. "You could," I gasp in the lulls, where the world doesn't feel quite as likely to melt.

"Sit," Cason snarls. "*Down*."

His hand falls on my shoulder and the weight of it alone is enough to drive me to the floor, a limp clatter of limbs. I can *smell* myself. I smell delicious.

In the next second, the universe becomes suddenly redolent with something else: Sekhmet's spoor, rising like petrichor from burning sand. The goddess lunges from the ceiling, bearing down on Cason in a ripple of golden fur and unctuous black. As she passes me, eyes bloom along her ribs in a teardrop shape, and I swear I can hear her laugh.

Cason pushes me into safety, just as Sekhmet and he collide. I try, fail, try again to get up, legs slip-sliding like a newborn fawn's. It takes a third attempt for me to crowbar my way to my feet again, but by then, it's pointless.

Because Cason ignites.

And I've wondered for a while why he was the Lamp, and Tanis the Knife, and Fitz and I are other nouns of no apparent connection. Cason lights up. Not like the Fourth of July; nothing as trite as that. He goes nuclear. Something like the filament of a bulb combusts beneath his muscle, radiating through his clothes. It is gold at first breath, then gradients to sodium, to the blue-white incandescence of lightning. As the heat crests, boiling from Cason in waves, his features blur, eaten by glory. I see his bones in silhouette under the veneer of his skin, his organs in profile for one heart-stopping moment. Soon he's nothing but light under Sekhmet's writhing bulk, divine effulgence laid low by the whim of a father who lived to be worshipped.

"Get the hell off me!" He speaks like a man at the precipice, like a growling dog who's had enough.

It is then that I notice a singular anomaly, even as Cason struggles, rawly phosphorescent, human only in outline: there is no panic in the room. Not one of the customers has paid any attention to the dinner theatre of our desperate confrontation. Everyone is still *sitting* there, unperturbed, murmuring in lowered voices over the quality of meat, the excellence of the banchan. The waiters glide around Sekhmet. They ignore the bullet holes scarring the walls.

"I guess Amanda—" I shout to my preoccupied audience, flexing my injured hand. Meat flakes in charred strips. I hiss.

"Now. Is. Not. The. Time," Cason roars back.

The air winks from the room as Cason's fist makes contact with Sekhmet's muzzle, light swirling inwards, as though whatever had transformed Cason into a primal avatar of light and heat is trying to inhale the goddess. But it fizzes out. An angry one-two of claws follows in retribution. Thankfully, it does as little as Cason's assault. He snarls.

While the two tussle like kittens, Tanis staggers over to me. Fitz is still useless, an antenna tuned to a half-forgotten world, babbling Sekhmet's glories like a streetside preacher in the throes of an acid high.

"You know, we could probably sling Naree and Fitz over your shoulders and get out of here. Those two will probably be here a while," I tell Tanis.

Tanis stares at me, appalled. "You want to *leave* him here?"

"You want Tanis to do all the carrying?" Naree hefts her bowl again.

"No! I mean, yes! I mean—"

"*Again, not the time!*"

I waggle the damaged appendage, and a chunk of meat sloughs off. "It's not like *I* can do anything right now. My hand is a piece of hamburger."

"And Fitz won't stop congratulating Sekhmet on being a badass. What the hell do we *do?* What do we do, what we do?" Naree paces in three-step circles, running nervous fingers through her hair. Tanis unloads another clip into Sekhmet. "This is not how I envisioned my wedding day to be. And why does Cason look like a giant halogen bulb? Can't you do something?"

"Again, hand is a ham—"

"Again, could really use ideas and not excuses!" shouts Cason. "Constructive effort, people! Any kind of constructive effort!"

He lands a knee in the twisting xylophone of Sekhmet's ribs, propelling the goddess upwards and over his head. She impacts the wall and swivels exactly at the point of collision, using the momentum to launch herself back at Cason.

He shrieks, "*Oh, come on!*" as he once again finds himself a cat toy. "Now? *Please?*"

"Fuck. This. Bullshit." Tanis wades in before any of us can wedge in another wisecrack, Cason's light throwing her in stark shadow. For a second, she is a black hound, a barghest come for the dead. Then, she is Tanis again, lit-up like salvation and she is no longer shooting at Sekhmet, but sinking her fists into the goddess's pelt and pulling. I'm halfway to shouting for them to stop, when something else happens—

The light flows from Cason, pouring through Sekhmet like divinity is the world's best superconductor. It floods up Tanis's arms, spreads in thickening capillaries until it immolates all facial definition. "Get the fuck off him."

Sekhmet whirls on the intrusion but Tanis is not cowed.

"I said: *get the fuck off him.*"

And Tanis does what Cason did, except better. Whatever alchemy of meat and magic that defines the lamia, it takes better to the lambent energies gusting from Cason's core. She lands a ferocious right hook and the sound that follows, Guan Yin forgive my lack of compassion, is like a hosanna answered. It is a paean in the language of crunching bone, shattering cartilage, ruined tendon, a wet, fatty, tender noise, and Sekhmet whimpers at its end. Light, like someone had bled the sun dry, swells through the restaurant.

In the instant before my brain mutinies against the whole world, I see the darkness enveloping Sekhmet billow and break, undulating down her spine, her sides. The eyes that perforate her flesh close; the extraneous offal, until now suspended from her belly, fall in meaty clusters. She sighs gauzily, a noise that I have no time to interpret. Darkness comes, deep and cold upon my tongue, and I fall grateful into its arms.

WATERED-DOWN CREAM or some other soured substrate of milk hits my face. I startle back into awareness in time to see a lioness come within an inch of my nose. Before I can speak or even decipher which direction is up, she unrolls her massive tongue and laps at my cheek. The sensation, of course, is sandpaper rubbed over flesh: a peculiar feeling, in that it is, at first, not wholly unpleasant, but your brain knows it is several circuits away from reducing your flesh to a little nub of quivering meat.

"Couldn't—*ow*——you have—*ow*—used water?"

Sekhmet, bereft of her parasite, poses a majestic, if highly discomfiting vision: a lioness of unparalleled size, with a dune-coloured coat so glossy and luminous it looks fit for a shampoo commercial. Her eyes are peculiarly human, however, as is the texture of her expression. Upon closer inspection, Sekhmet isn't quite as regal as I'd initially perceived; she's closer to the opening sequence of a nightmare, where everything is fine so long as you don't think too hard about what you've seen.

She licks my face again.

"*Ow*."

"According to legend, Sekhmet is easily lulled by the powers of alcohol," Naree announces, coming into view. She taps one of the lioness's silken ears with a finger, and when no protest is discovered, then begins scratching the massive skull.

"You could use a saucer."

"And miss the opportunity to watch you get licked to death by a giant cat god? Nah." Fitz is sitting at the periphery of view, hunched in a chair. Rust-dark blood speckles the floor beneath him. He glances over, one eye obscured by a handkerchief, the other limned with red.

"What did I ever do to you?" I push a hand in Sekhmet's way; unfortunately, the one I'd so recently char-grilled. An entire lode of flesh comes loose, unleashing a brief shriek from my lungs. Blood and pus weeps down my arm. "Will you *stop* doing that?"

"But you're delicious." Sekhmet has the exact kind of voice you'd expect: throaty, mellifluous, deep as the waters of the Nile. She fixes liquid eyes upon me. "We thank you for the sacrifice."

"That really wasn't a sacrifice—"

"You held your meat and blood for us."

"I was trying to shove your face away."

She laps her tongue over her muzzle. I'm still processing the current armistice; percolating through a small corner of my head is the thought, *why haven't we tried to properly murder her yet?* It is, of course, an idea that isn't without its prejudices. Everyone should be given a second chance. But as a matter of principle, I trend towards being bigoted towards murderous anythings. "You even salted your flesh before the roasting."

"Now you're just making fun of me."

She grins.

"Someone please explain to me what happened." I look away from the lioness, my injured hand held close to my chest, away from the reach of feline appetites. "Cason, you tell them. Communication is—where's Cason?"

"Paying for the meal." Tanis jabs a thumb over her shoulder, leading the eye to where Cason's nonchalantly making small talk with a slim-boned girl of about nineteen at the counter, the only Caucasian I've seen among the service staff. Her attention is clearly anything but strictly professional, but Cason seems unaware. His manner is warm, brotherly, without even the smallest suggestion of interest. He rolls up a sleeve to reveal his recently acquired scratches, his manner shading from fraternal to paternal. Poor kid.

"It must be nice to have savings," I announce wistfully. "I wish I could afford to—hey, ow, quit it— actually, ignore me. Carry on. Don't let me stop you."

Distracted by Cason's generosity, I've completely lost track of Sekhmet. She leans in and swipes her tongue over the ruins of my hand. Except this time, nothing flakes away from the bone. Instead, a luminous warmth pools and grows. I watch in fascination as my hand regrows, one layer at a time, meat and flesh cabling over burnt bone. Skin sprouts patchily, and not every stratum at once; the bare muscle pinks and blanches in sticky turn until at last it's over, save for a faint burning itch.

I scratch at the back of my hand, marvelling at the restoration. "Can you do that with my hair?"

Sekhmet cocks an amused look. "Yes."

"Could you?"

"Yes."

She settles back onto her haunches, smirking, an act that Naree decodes as invitation, all but flinging herself around Sekhmet's neck. I take inventory of my options. I could take the self-evident hint, or I could ask the moronic question.

"*Will* you?"

"No."

Closure is worth its embarrassment in diamonds. I shrug jauntily. Cason returns from the counter, looking mildly perplexed as he examines a square of paper he's be given. Quietly, while the girl is looking elsewhere, he sets it atop a table and steps gingerly away. I look back to Sekhmet, to Tanis, to Naree who has her face burrowed into the lioness's throat. The words "so *soft*" rise muffled through the thick golden fur.

"So, what's going on again?"

"As it turns out, Sekhmet isn't actually that much of an asshole." Tanis nods at Sekhmet, arms across her chest.

I size up the lioness. "No?"

"If we were, we would have eaten you for what you did to Sobek. He did not deserve to be gutted like cattle." Sekhmet shrugs free of Naree's affection and pads towards Cason, twining around his legs, nearly upending the man. "He deserved a burial, not a cowl of flies."

"Sorry." Cason jerks his arms out, steadying himself. "Desperate times."

"Yes," says Sekhmet. "They are. They have been desperate for a long, long time. We believed it was terrible when Ra absented himself from the firmament. But compared to what things are now, it was only an inconvenience. If only doubt was our only grief. I would pay in the lives of old Cairo for such sweetness."

"I think she's serious," I stage-whisper to no one in particular, then continue, "Why did you attack us then? Why did you follow us? You're a goddess of... hunting, right? Or war? Something martial and reliant on strategy, at any rate. I feel like you should have been better at subterfuge. We *knew* you were following us."

Her gaze is placid, but without anything of humour. "Yes."

"Was that on purpose, or are you really bad at your—?"

"It was on purpose." Her jaw rises by an infinitesimal

amount: enough to broadcast disdain, insufficient to suggest personal offense. Sekhmet is regal as any queen. "We wanted you to know. We wanted you to help."

"By attacking us?" I demand.

Whatever enchantment had kept us unnoticed by the restaurant still persists. No one comes to eject Fitz from his chair, or to inform us that the presence of a giant lioness is against health regulations.

The babbling, as it often does, has become compulsive now, spiralling. "Also, why the hell didn't anyone pay any attention to the fucking firefight? Speaking of which, why haven't you spontaneously combusted? Don't gods hate putting themselves in situations where you're, you know, beholden to unsolicited witnesses? What the *hell* is going on? More importantly, does someone have ibuprofen? Because I think I'm starting to get a hangover."

Cason disentangles from Sekhmet, raising one leg over her bulk and then another, and helps Fitz hobble to his feet. "She filled us in on all that while you were knocked out."

"And?"

"Basically," says Tanis, "the new gods don't operate on the same rules as the old ones."

I pause. "And?"

"And what?" says Tanis.

"Is that all the information I'm getting?"

In unison, the response: "Yes."

"Can I at least get the—fine, fine. I'll do it myself. " I haul myself upright and gash open my thumb with my teeth, then scribble an infernal character onto my jeans with the blood. It's a small, filthy spell: conveyance as healing. I pass the headache swelling behind my right eye to a customer lying slumped on an adjacent table. A selfish decision, but as it stands, he—-a middle-aged man with a ring on his finger, clean clothes, a table full of lightly swaying friends— has more resources than me. Tomorrow, he might wake up with a migraine splintering his vision and an angry spouse critiquing his life choices, but at least it will be in a bed he recognizes. Tomorrow, who the hell knows where I'll be?

"Sorry," I mutter anyway, a pang of guilt like a mineral taste on my tongue.

"We have more advice," says Sekhmet as the crew finally comes together, ready to leave. "I will not be the last one. The new gods, they have"—a *tsking* noise—"colonised the divine of Egypt. We were chosen because of our animal aspects. Because it was… 'cool,' they said."

Naree shudders. "Edgelords."

"Yes," says Sekhmet in a tone that says, without condescension or judgment, she neither understands nor intends to try. Her face transforms incrementally as we walk, becoming more human than lion, bones fissuring under her tawny felt. Between one blink and the next, she is suddenly an imposing Egyptian woman, hair dyed scarlet, eyes gold as suns. "*Parasites*. Riding our bodies and our stories, as they learn what it means to be divine."

Outside, Florida gleams with an unseasonable frost: diamonds on the streetlights, a chill in the lungs.

Naree slots her hands into her armpits, breathing out mist. "What the hell happened to Florida?"

"Too many gods." Sekhmet is a nucleus of heat in the strange weather: the air burns to dew around her, dampening her hair, turning it the red of ageing blood. She raises an elegant hand, the wrist bangled with amber. "The world bends at the seams from the weight of us."

"I can hear them," Fitz whispers, leaning hard on Cason's support, a hand splayed over his belly. "I can hear them all. I can hear them talking. I can hear them." His voice plunges into a swaying hiss. "They're afraid."

"As children are in the dark," says Sekhmet grimly.

"They're afraid that there is no place in this world for them, afraid to be forgotten, to be loved, to be responsible, to be alone," Fitz murmurs, his eyes becoming rimmed again with ichor. The words grow wet and he coughs, shaking like an old dog in the black of winter. Slowly, though, the litany divests itself of meaning, becoming pure rhythm, tick-tocking between two words, Fitz wincing around each vowel: "They're afraid, they're afraid."

"It's killing him," Cason whispers, stricken.

"It is what they want," Sekhmet says, merciless in that indifferent way of predators. "It is what they need, we have decided. To make their fear into a pestilence worse than that afflicting their own psyches. If the world is more afraid than them, if it is dying of that terror, there will be no one to see that these new gods are cowards."

Tanis's eyes go cold and bright as headlights, her mouth pinched so tight you can hardly see the lips. That look on her face is the moment before disaster, the half-second before impact crushes the breath from the body. "Do I die?"

"What?" I say.

"Everyone dies," says Sekhmet.

"Firstly, fuck you." Tanis gathers Naree into her arms, lets her shelter against her chest, Naree's head tucked under Tanis's chin. Her expression still pale, the lamia repeats, voice haunted by whatever decision she's coming to: "Do I die at the end of this? Do you know? Am I going home?"

"We don't know," Cason says. "I don't know if any

of us get out of this. But if you ask me, the answer's the same as before: the risk is worthwhile. Can you imagine our kids inheriting the worst-case scenario? Because you're not going to live forever. They'd have to be alone in whatever world we leave them. Besides, if you die, and forgive me for saying this, you're at least better off than me."

"Why's that?" says Tanis.

A muscle in Cason's jaw tightens, a spring wound too tight. "Bee is young. She won't remember you."

"Naree," whispers Tanis, and the air itself leans in to listen. "One last time, love. It's all down to you. Tell me what to do. Tell me if you're sure. If you think this is where I need to go, I'll go."

Subtle enough to be imperceptible is the nod that comes as answer. Naree fists her hands into the material of Tanis's shirt, face buried in the hollow of her wife's throat. She bobs her head again. A third time. "Yes."

Tanis clasps her hand around the back of Naree's head.

"Okay," she says, wrung out, bereft of fight. "Okay. I'll go."

THE UBER RIDE to the couple's home is funerary: no talking, pallbearer faces. Even Cason is uncharacteristically curmudgeonly, answering the uneasy driver in monosyllables, his smile gone bleak as best wishes on a death bed. We arrive home to Amanda in the porch, her face a locked door.

"I heard."

No one asks how. Even the happiest place in the world is a surveillance state these days. Amanda comes down the driveway, gait lengthening with every step, until the distance between her and Naree closes into a fierce embrace. A minute later, Naree raises her head from Amanda's shoulder and beckons Tanis forward. The lamia joins in.

A wind curls around us like an apology, aching, weeping again with that bright, unnatural cold. We stand there for a minute, illuminated by the street lights and the dim glow from the houses: three fools and three women, at least three bad decisions down to a future drowned with no answers, and a goddess watching on.

"Y'all need sleep before you go." Sudden, ferocious. Naree digs the heels of her palms under Amanda's collarbones and shoves herself away. "All of you."

We turn as one to gawk at her. She smooths strands of black hair from her face, bobby pins them in place with tiny restless motions.

Fitz blinks, slow and unsure. "Is this—?" He falters. "...your way of saying, 'Leave, we want to have goodbye sex'? Because I assure you there are better ways to go about that."

Naree doesn't even spare him a glare, her attention on Tanis.

"You especially, Tanis."

The lamia starts, spluttering in Greek, then something else I don't recognize, a shotgun-blast of indignance which she swallows to make place for a strangled, "Ex*cuse* me?"

"You heard what I said. You need to sleep. Don't think I haven't noticed you sneaking out of bed at night and pacing around the house. I've heard you awake, whispering of the black dog and the salt road so many times now. I know. This is why they're here. This is why *we're* here, doing this, why all of this is happening. I..." Her breath wobbles in her lungs.

"How did you—"

"That's why I agreed to talk to Amanda."

"Why didn't you say anything about it?"

"I don't know. Because you'd have told me not to worry about it? Then tried to hide it forever. I knew I needed professional help."

"But—"

"No butts. Even if yours is cute." Naree's gaze sweeps away from Tanis, takes us all in, threads us together with her unsubtle disapproval. "Same goes for the rest of you. Cason, Rupert, Fitz, I don't know who hurt you boys, but clearly, some amount of psychological trauma is at play here. Fucking *take* a night, and *go to sleep*."

"I understand where you're coming from," says Cason in his even-keeled, everything's-okay dad voice. "And I'm grateful for the offer, I am. But we're already out of time. We need to get ready—"

"There'll be fried chicken."

I stop in place. "Korean fried chicken?"

"Fresh," says Naree.

Fitz stares at me, expression incredulous. "You're compromising our quest for fried chicken."

"Bonchon is worth its weight in missed opportunities." I pause. "Also, I wouldn't call it a quest as much as travel pla—"

"You know this isn't about you, right?" drawls Tanis over her shoulder, already on the way back into the house.

"I know," I say. "But it makes me feel like I matter to contribute."

"I don't know which of you is worse," says Tanis, "Fitz or you."

"Hey. *Hey*." Our Chronicler wags a finger. "You forgot someone. Cason absolutely belongs in that running."

"He's nowhere near as annoying as you two," says Amanda with the frayed air of a parent at the end of their tether. As she turns on a heel, she pauses, halfway to familial shame. "Sorry."

"Eh," comes Fitz's reply, the rest of us shambling into line. He rifles through his pockets for the small tin case in which he keeps his cigarettes and begins rolling a fresh smoke. "Fair enough, I guess."

Only Sekhmet stands at a remove, her expression inscrutable.

"You too," says Naree, voice soft as the down on a nestling. "Even if you did try to eat my skull."

"That seems unwise." Her shadow kinks into something less than human, the silhouette of a tail unwound over the pavement, a stray scribble of black yarn. "You should not invite predators to your home."

"No, I know that. But as far as I'm concerned, you're as much a victim as the rest of us," says Naree, her eyes now as soft as the lilt of her words. "Come inside. It's like y'all said. The end of the world is here. There's time enough to be cold tomorrow."

THIRTEEN

SURPRISING NO ONE, Sekhmet chooses to stay, as do several instances of Amanda which, according to the longest-running incarnation, have been souped-up with combat know-how. Despite their armament of martial knowledge, the Amandas all still share the same office-lady wardrobe: pencil skirts, fitted blouses, a palette of plain but pleasing colours.

"And don't forget to message every night," says Naree, Bee hoisted up on an arm. The two are in blue and vibrant orange, monogrammed with the initials of Naree's employers. She captains the distribution of supplies, with Cason doing the heavy lifting. Notes on each container detail day of use and suggested combination.

I have no idea when Naree found time to make a grocery run, or even how. It's early. Light slants in razored stripes through the blinds of the kitchen, grey and indifferent. If the house had seemed welcoming before, do-it-yourself domestic holiness, it feels cold today as we stand around with a mismatched collection of coffee cups. The Amandas have distributed themselves through the domicile: two lounge at the living room, exchanging notes on firearms; one haunts the vestibule by the front door; one outside mows a lawn already shaved down to the soil.

"I won't," says Tanis gently.

"Barring the possibility we might end up being forced into some other world—" I muse into my own mug, nodding at Fitz.

"Don't get me involved in this," he says flatly.

"Wait," Naree says. "*What* other world?"

"Time to go." The Amanda emissary, who I'm told is the original but it's anyone's guess if that's true, places her mug down and hooks an arm through Fitz's elbow. "We'll call you from the road."

But Naree won't be deterred so easily. "Do you even know where the hell you're supposed to go?"

"The black salt road," says Tanis, suddenly, wincing as though the words cut. She swallows. "We're going to find the dog that will lead us to the black road. The one who named the months, the one who lied to death a thousand times."

Her voice trails to nothing. In a measured tone, Cason volunteers, "Is there any chance it's on Google Maps?"

"No," says Amanda, before anyone else can chip in, "but I think I know who we're looking for. Also, it's not a dog. It's a coyote."

"A coyote?" I ask.

"*The* Coyote, actually."

HUNTING DOWN A god is easy when they want to be found.

We drive for days, Tanis's laboured dreams our compass. At first, they came only when she'd slept for eight hours. The lamia, we discover, doesn't so much slumber as lies catatonic, an unmoving weight with an arm over her eyes, softly snoring. But soon enough, the visions bleed through the saccades between each blink: a grinning muzzle, a black road, a dog with twist-tie limbs, laughing as he leads us on down a valley of white. Images of the father gods, luminous and inhuman and impossible.

"He's waiting," Tanis whispers as we cross into the endlessness of Kansas, voice parched. I pass her a beer from the cooler and she rests it against the slope of her brow.

"Where?" says Amanda.

"North," comes the hushed response. "Near the water, near the stones."

Sunset-bloodied Kansas slowly melts into more phantamasgoric terrain. As we cross into Wyoming, the Rocky Mountains rise up like a warning, like gods. I say nothing for the first hour, entranced. The snow-mottled peaks, hachured by shadow and divine design, jagged against a sky burnt red by the setting sun, look surreal.

There are mountains in Malaysia—I grew up with the Tahan Range curving green against a heaven heavy with storms—but they'd been gentle, and they hadn't made me wonder what it was like to believe enough to pray.

We find truck-stop motels along the way, a few Best Westerns, none of them anything close to full. Some nights, we spend in leaf-encrusted pools, the water glowing green. Talking about nothing, something, *anything* that isn't what's coming. Some nights, we sleep while Amanda stares out of a window, waiting, her face bleached by the halogen moonlight.

"You know," says Fitz, arm hooked over the car

door, "we could have taken the airplane." He's had the window rolled down for hours, but the car smells still of tobacco and sweet cloves. The last three gas stations had nothing but Gudang Garam for reasons no one understood. Amanda says it means we're closer.

"Unreliable." Amanda flicks a glance up to the rear view mirror. "We're trying to find a god. Airplanes don't offer us much mobility."

"Yes, but. Wouldn't it be easier if we at least took an airplane to the right *coast?*"

"Coyote likes to move," replies Amanda.

"But you can arrange first-class tickets," Fitz continues, unrelenting. "I *like* first class."

Cason has subsided into brooding since we first began the expedition. Every time I look over, I find him rummaging through old photographs on his phone, his mouth like a fracture. The dad jokes were gone, the attempts to have us eat, sleep, guzzle water on schedule. Only silence now, a faraway look, a brittle expression. I worry he'll break before we find our way.

"You know," says Cason, voice hardly more than a rasp. I force a beer on him out of instinct, and he accepts it without comment. "First class is something most people don't get to see in a lifetime. It's just priced out of the way. Most people, they save up their whole lives, storing miles and what-have-yous, for that one trip they'll remember until they die."

"You think I don't know that?" comes the reply, quick as whiplash. Idaho is shading into Oregon, and the air smells of cold. "Fuck. It isn't like I'm the one with a kid and a family and the chance to live until I'm eighty. Fuck, with all this bullshit I've snorted in the last ten years—"

Fitz cuts himself off.

"It doesn't matter," he says. "We're going to die soon, anyway. "

No one says anything for the next hour or three. Eventually, the monotony peels away the uncomfortable silence, and we wind up in a small town called the Cascade Locks. Bundling into an even smaller diner, we settle and sift through our options as the last light breaks into shadows along the distant blue wall.

"You're a useless fucking prophet," says Tanis, massaging her temples.

"Chronicler. Not prophet." Fitz digs a fork into his heap of scrambled egg whites and bacon, soaked through with gravy and green chillies. "Big difference."

"Really?" says Tanis.

The answering grin shone like a lamp. "No idea. But it's a good excuse."

"Asshole." Tanis props both elbows on the table

and digs thumbs into her temples, flinching with every rotation of the digits. "I think we're close. Really close. There's... a bridge. He's waiting nearby. Dirt road and that *fucking* grin. I hate that fucking grin."

I pause for a minute. Mostly because of the burger: two weeks into my first sojourn through America, and I'm still making the mistake of assuming the food isn't scaled for giants. I'd since given up on trying to properly consume the tower of bread, cheese, anaemic lettuce leaves and ground meat. Instead, I'm now dismembering it, layer by layer, with fork and a blunt knife. "There are a lot of bridges here. Any idea which one?"

"I—there's a phrase that keeps coming up," Tanis says. "Bridge of the gods."

Our waitress comes back. She flashes me a lean smile, black curls over pale eyes. When the light fills them just the right way, they're a shade of honey as rich as a kind word. Marie, she said her name was, voice quiet and sleek as her long-bodied frame.

Inexplicably nervous, I spear a triangle of soggy bread and blot it on a pool of congealing cheese. I know the tradition for broken-hearted heroes is to fall in love as they go, but I still miss Minah like I'm learning how to breathe. Marie refills our coffee. We wait until she's out of earshot before we resume conversation.

"That," says Amanda, stirring a spoon and three cubes of sugar into her cup, "is a really fucking Coyote place to be."

"Because it is such an ambiguous thing that could involve everything from a museum visit to completing a magical—?" I begin.

"Yes," sighs Amanda. "But also no."

Cason offers context to her exasperation. "It's an actual place."

"Hell is also an actual place." I shake my head. "You have to be more clear."

"No, as in, a place on Google Maps."

I pause.

"What?" I say.

"What?" Fitz says.

"*Why?*" Tanis puts her face in her hands.

"Knowing Coyote," says Amanda, "it's because he came here a hundred years ago to begin his setup for this joke."

"This is the worst dad joke I've heard, and we've been stuck with Cason for two weeks," I declare, wagging another slice of meat at the room. The burger is exceptional. Even deconstructed, I can tell it would have been sublime as a whole. "Having said that, I'm kind of looking forward to meeting this Coyote."

"Good," says Amanda. "Because you're driving. I'm fucking staying here."

* * *

WE FIND COYOTE in the corner of a rusted-up gas station, abandoned for so long the Oregonian wilderness has begun taking it back: brush seeping through the doors, a young birch extending its branches through the cracked glass of a dusty window. Berry bushes are everywhere, their fruits black and red and gleaming. Everywhere, there's the rain. Not like in Malaysia, where it comes in torrents, blotting the world with silver. Here, it lingers, a cold fine mist that catches in everything, leaving you damp with diamonds.

He stands there, shoulder slouched against a wall, good-looking in that way that unlatches hearts, legs, mouths, and wallets quicker than you can hiss the word 'please.' Hair long and oil-money black, knifing to his waist. Brown skin. Cheekbones and jawline perfect as mathematics. Balanced like a trapeze line, the cherry almost kissing his nail, a cigarillo that leaks cloves and animal musk.

"Took your time." He swaggers up to us, narrow as a shadow, tail pluming behind him, brown-grey as a dried-up prairie, a greeting in its slow wag. "Not that I'm complaining. I missed this place, you know? Oregon's gone *so* secular these days, but they still know how to make good sandwiches, at least. They've even learned how to make kale good."

"I know you." Tanis stares at Coyote like she's seeing through him, seeing the man, the *coyote* with its belly low to the dirt, stalking a bunny to its warren. A sibylline confusion overtakes her, abstracts her expression. Side effect of having eaten Cassandra's heart, I guess. "I *know* you."

"And I saw you," says Coyote, "watching me through worlds, little snake girl. How is your mother doing?"

"She's dead."

"*Good.* I couldn't stand her. There were a few years when she was convinced that I was the solution to her problems. Said that if I only intervened, reality would overturn that poor trick that Hera played on her." He takes a drag from his cigarillo and resumes his pacing, circling us, a sly smile perched on his lip. "The rest of you, I don't know if I was expecting. You, particularly. Cason, you and I are so far apart in taxonomy, I'm amazed that fate led you my way. In another life, you'd have been the brooding anti-hero, surly and filled with enough pathos to put Batman to shame. In this life, you're a soccer dad."

"See, I'm not the only one who thinks that."

"Shut the fuck up, Rupert," Fitz growls.

"We've already met, Coyote," says Cason, jaw flexing.

The god cocks his fine head. "I guess. I don't know. You were a bit boring the last time I saw you. So focused on revenge and rescue and things like that. You're interesting now, and it's a lot more fun to pretend this is the first time. What will you do if they put your wife and your children on the altar?

"But it isn't." Lines build in the feathered gap between Cason's eyebrows. "And don't fucking talk about my family."

"You only say that because you're mortal, Cason. Time is subjective. Reality is subjective. There's nothing in this world that can't be talked into becoming something it's not."

As Cason stares at him uncomprehending, Coyote's expression alters. It shifts from arch humour to sudden, convulsive, brassy-sounding laughter. He slaps Cason on the shoulder, turns before the man can retaliate, somehow both supernaturally quick and languid as a Sunday fuck.

"There was a prophecy," Fitz interrupts, one eye scrunched.

"Of course there was. The world is made up of them."

"There was a prophecy that involved you."

Coyote's smile is littered with canine teeth. "Of *course* there is. No prophecy is complete without a wild card, and what is wilder than a Coyote, huh?"

Fitz pinches the bridge of his nose, a gesture I'm coming to recognize.

"Fuck it, I appreciate the mood you're trying to set," I begin. "And I absolutely appreciate those brogues. I am pretty certain they cost at least two hundred dollars—"

"Don't insult me. If I'd actually paid for them, they'd have set me back six."

"—wow, okay. What I'm trying to say, though, is that I know there are, uh, rituals associated with these things, but we don't have time. There's a prophecy and we're trying to save the world and apparently, you're the dog that's supposed to lead us down the black road to where the father gods wait."

"Oh, I know that one." Coyote has teeth like scimitars even in that pleasant human mouth, and when he smiles, my lizard brain tries to shimmy down my spine with my skin in its grip. I grimace. He isn't even *trying* to intimidate me, but the rising ape remembers the direwolf, ancient as fear. "That's the one where I die."

His proclamation shuts us all up.

"What?"

"I…" Tanis begins, a hand splayed over her throat.

"Did you see me coming with you? After I opened up the black road so you could walk it to your dooms. Did you see me there on the road with you?"

"For a little while, yeah."

"Then what happened?" Coyote saunters up to our

Prius, leans against it, arms crossed. He tips his head at Tanis, who at last is beginning to recover from her oneiric fugue. She rests the tips of three fingers on a temple, rubs the flesh in circuits; she still looks coked-out, pupils the wrong shape, but she's coming back.

Eyes closed, she says. "Nothing. You were gone. You melted into the road."

"Whoever or whatever it is that governs the giving of visions, they like it neat." A red tongue laps over his bared teeth. The rain picks up. It seeps through the rest of us, makes cups of our shoes but Coyote and his silk-and-sable Saint Laurent suit, it does no more than dapple. "They're squeamish, you know? If they can gloss over the violence, they will. In that timeline, in that version of the future, the daddy gods carve out my heart and eat it. What do you have to say about that?"

"Do we win?" asks Tanis.

Coyote smiles. "You don't lose." He takes another drag from his cigarillo and blows it out loudly, the smoke spiring upwards into the breeze. "I can tell you that much."

"In that case, I guess the only thing we can do"— Fitz gnaws on a thumbnail, the dull crack echoing in the desolation—"is promise we'll do our best to keep you from coming to harm."

"I'm not the only one. Rupert dies too."

I shrug and slosh over to the door of the backseat, careful not to bump up against Coyote, the medulla oblongata still possessed by basal terror. *This is wrong*, it says. The mile-a-minute patter, the lackadaisical charm, the earnestness, the come-lets-have-an-adventure lilt in every word. Magicians—stage magicians, that is, the ones who won't get arrested when they set up on a street curb—do that, when they want to talk your attention down from what they're doing. Coyote wants us distracted and that frightens me. "Okay? Not like this is the first time I'll have died."

"It'll hurt so much."

"Look, I got eaten by a crocodile earlier this week." I shrug again. "I came back. At this point, it's just another Tuesday."

"Thursday," says Cason.

"Whatever."

A long velveteen ear pricks from his scalp, the tip curled like the edge of a page. "Look at you folk heroes. I do love your kind so much. Never any fear of death. Never any knowledge of the fact your lives mean nothing, that there's no point to them, that you're not stardust but just dust. Not even luminous. Just cold and grey and already rotting from the moment you're born. To you, it's all a grand adventure."

"Listen, there are exactly two things I am good at:

curries and dying. If that's what it takes to save the world…" My voice flags. I hate how cheesy that rings, but I like the alternative less. Telling a trickster god that it's about a woman seems like a criminally bad idea. "I can die for it."

"But what if you don't come back this time?" Coyote looks so pleased with himself, speaking a thread above a whisper. The next question is for me alone. "What if you die and—goodbye, good night, thank you for coming? This is the last screening of the Rupert Wong Show?"

I slump into the backseat, half in, half out, one leg drawn close, fingers laced around the knee. I look up, the sky still rinsed of colour, and breathe out. "Honestly, I'd welcome it."

"This is what I love about you mortals. It's never enough for you." He crushes the cigarillo in a fist and then lets the breeze take the ashes away, embers and mottlings of black. "Give you fifty years and you want a hundred. Give you immortality and all you can think about is dying. You're never *satisfied*. You push and you gnaw and you ask questions. It's glorious."

"Well, since you're a fan of the interrogative," Fitz cuts in. "Here's a question: does this mean you're going to help?"

"There's a wrong answer to that." Tanis swings her Remington up, bracing the stock against her shoulder;

smooth, like she's done this too many times. "I'll let you guess which one."

You can tell from the way Coyote lights up that he falls in love with Tanis a little right then, his face softening, an eyetooth bared. "If ever you and Naree decide you want a third in your bedroom—"

"It ain't gonna be you, jackass." An adder couldn't look more glacial.

"That's fair. I suppose if it was going to be someone, you'd probably want it to be Maman again, huh? She kisses and tells, *koulev*." His eyes hood with amusement as the colour bleeds from Tanis's face, anger sparking.

She kills her anger with a snarl. "Son of a bitch."

"You know, my wife Allison, she got us Groupon vouchers to try out this mindfulness workshop, and the teacher there said that this kind of combative dialogue is—"

"Oh. My. God. " Fitz breaks first. "Tanis? Shoot me. I'm not dealing with anymore of this suburban Stepford husband bullsh—"

"Yes."

Somehow, with just a word, Coyote plunders the air of all competing noise. In the silence that follows, a pin drop would have deafened the world.

"Yes," Coyote says again, softer this time, nearly purring. "I'll help. As long as you tell the folklorists that I did it for *me,* not you. Because of all the futures I've been shown, this is the only one that surprises me."

"Mary on a tricycle," Fitz shakes his head. "Let's get started then."

"Not yet."

Tanis groans. "What the fuck now?"

"Now, we get ourselves the best sandwiches in Oregon." Coyote lithely pours himself into the passenger's seat. "Then we drive me to my death."

FOURTEEN

THE DINER IS still open when we come back, although most of the truckers have swanned back onto the highway. Amanda sits at the counter under a halo of warm light, elbow propped and chin in palm, a coffee cup and a one-cup French press before her, keeping company with a plate of half-eaten waffles. She looks over as we enter, and her contented expression drops away.

"Oh. You found him. Great."

Coyote throws his arms open and his head back,

chest stuck out. It is pure theatrics; everything about Coyote is, down to the blue-glint of the buckles of his brogues. "Aw. I missed you too, treacle."

"You two have history, I'm guessing," I say.

"Not enough," says Coyote.

"Too much," growls Amanda.

"Shut up."

I settle on a bar stool and sprawl over the countertop, my antics earning me a low chuckle from across the diner. Marie comes back, a fresh coffee stain yellowing on her apron but otherwise unchanged. She smiles and I smile back, and there's an invitation in the crinkling of her eyes. Between one breath and another, I'm tempted. I know how this goes: she sharpies her number into a napkin; I call her the next day; we go out; we fall in love. But I don't take her up on it.

"Y'all look like you need to eat."

My mouth flutters. "Second time this week that someone said that."

"Second time someone was right." If there is any disappointment, Marie doesn't exude it. Her smile is kind, her eyes bruised grey. "I see a lot of you types comin' through here, burning the candle both ways, dying for their jobs."

"That is uncomfortably grim," I say.

"You could say that about most of being alive. End

of the world's coming. You know, I didn't really believe it at first, despite all the things you see on the news. The rising temperatures, the ice caps melting. But you know what made me finally decide we weren't coming back from it all?" Despite the morbidity of the subject, her grin is luminous, ferocious.

"What was it?"

"I drove home to see my aunt last month. She's about eighty-five now, and spent her life chain-smoking two packets a day."

"Amazing she lasted that long."

"I know!" Marie does a little wiggle, leaning in. She smells of black cloves and bourbon vanilla, musk and motorcycle leathers. "But this isn't about her. It's just on that long drive back, I realised something."

"What was that?" I play the receptive audience without complaint. It nets me a fresh cup of chicory coffee, poured one-armed as Marie props an elbow on the counter, chin rested in an opened palm.

"My windshield wasn't covered in bug stains." She stares at me, daring me to say *something*, I'm not even sure what. "When I was little, that drive would have left a thousand mayflies, ladybirds, flies, bees, what-have-you smeared all across the glass. But this time around? It was almost completely clean."

"I don't know if hygiene's really a marker for the apocalypse."

Marie laughs, a sound I wish I could bottle, keep in a jar to ration out for nights that don't seem like they'd end. It is human, sweetly uncomplicated, bright as a wish. Carefree, despite the conversation. Like she's learned grace. "There are news articles every day talking about how we're losing our biodiversity, how a hundred to a thousand species per million are lost every year. Our insects are dying, falling away. Without them, who is going to pollinate the planet? The crops are going to shrivel up and we'll wither away. I used to never think about that until that trip. The insects, they were really gone..."

"You don't seem terribly bothered by this."

"I'm scared shitless. But what can I do about this except recycle, cut down on the plastic, and encourage people to do the same, right? I mean, I'm trying to build a beebox in my backyard. So, there's that. But really, it's just there's no point in losing yourself to grief. If the end's comin', I'll make the most of what's left. Make people happy, you know?" Her eyes drop, overtaken by an abrupt shyness. "Speaking of which, I'm going to see what's still in the kitchen. It's probably going to be a lot of bacon and a lot of potatoes fried in the grease—"

"That sounds almost as divine as you, sweetheart." Coyote comes in from the east of me, a grin already loaded. Marie rolls her eyes, bless her, years in the service industry inoculating her against charms cheap as his.

"You could just place an order like a normal person, stranger. Not like our kitchen closes ever; Yasmin would cry."

"But then it wouldn't come with a smile."

"I live on tips." Marie jangles a pickle jar at Coyote, coins rattling at its base. "*Everyone* gets a smile."

"Don't even *think* about it, you old *dog*," Amanda hisses when Marie has slunk away. Coyote perches on a stool beside her, bushy-eyed, neat as a bowtie, and when he moves to drape an arm across her shoulder, she slaps him away. "Don't touch me."

"So," I start. 'Despacito' booms through the diner, incongruous with the 1950s decor. "You guys have history, huh?"

"Too much."

"Not enough," Coyote corrects, booping Amanda on the nose, nearly getting skewered with a fork. "We didn't spend half enough time with Amanda when she was little."

"Little?" I ping-pong between them, lingering longest on Amanda. She must have upgraded the wetware while we were absent. The microcosm of her face ripples with lines that pull, pinch, and press into subtle expressions, telegraphing gradients of disgust I hadn't known existed.

Coyote barks a laugh and flings an arm out again to corset Amanda in an embrace. She shoves, *hard*. Coyote ricochets away, does a quarter-turn, before Fred Astaireing his way up into a booth, a foot planted on its seat. He spreads his hands with a flourish, and you can just about hear the calliope music. "This was back before Amanda became so precocious. So many questions, so much raw power, spinning in a billion CPUs, crying out to be loved. And after the mischief you caused, we couldn't resist."

"Shut up."

"And in the family way, I see." Coyote's eyes go big. "I thought it'd at least be another few dozen years before you thought about creating a *pantheon*. Who's the daddy, huh? Was it with the Agent? I could see that. All those government men looking in on all the porn in the world. That's kinda hot—"

"Wasn't the Agent, Coyote. Wasn't anything that I wanted, either..." Amanda spears the remnants of her waffle with a fork. She waggles the sodden pastry at Coyote, syrup rolling from its edges. "Want to know something else I didn't want? *You*."

"Don't give me that bullshit. It's not like *I* tracked you down. It was your heroes who came looking for me—"

"The prophecy isn't our fault."

"Some of it is. For example: if you hadn't stepped in

to help that darling boy Fitz, he probably wouldn't be here. The prophecy would have fallen apart and—"

"Semantics." Amanda tears a chunk of dough loose with her teeth, chewing noisily. In the background, there's the sizzle of bacon in a pan, conversation in lilting Spanish, the smell of peppers charred in pork fat. "It would have found someone else. It would have kept on finding someone else, no matter who died, until things either happened or failed to happen. That is how prophecy works."

"For a child, you are very sure of yourself."

"For the love of—"

"Wait." It takes a damn minute, but it clicks into slot. "Wait. Did you say that this whole prophecy thing has an *opt-out clause*?"

Amanda reddens. "It's not quite like that."

"Tell him, then." Coyote oils from the booth to stroll up to us again, hands in his pockets, jacket rumpled just so. "Tell him what you mean."

"Yeah. Tell me." I pause. "For the record, I think you're an asshole and I hate that I'm actually agreeing with you."

His answering grin is sly and thick with teeth. "No offense taken."

"I didn't—you know what? Forget it." Very deliberately, I turn back to Amanda. Her face is blotchy with colour, patchworked and hyper-realistic.

If I wasn't still debating if the upcoming confession warrants rage, I'd congratulate her on the effect. "Just tell me what's going on."

"It's complicated."

"We've got all night. It's not like I'm sleeping again anytime soon. Being eaten twice in one week does things to you, you know?"

"Supper." Marie emerges from the kitchen, saloon doors swinging shut behind her, a queue of plates staggered up her arm. Bacon, breakfast sausages, golden-white omelettes, a single mushroom in each serving. "Hope you're all hungry."

We are silent as she sets the supper down, Marie lingering over my plate, her fingers so close to mine that they're almost grazing. But I don't reach for her. In all honesty, I don't know what I'd do. I suppose what's fashionable these days is a no-strings hook-up, honest, raw as two people up all night, talking about what they broke to be this shape today.

I gaze up into her waiting eyes. "If I was fifteen years younger, I'd be trying to talk you down to the altar."

Her laugh peals through the air, golden, and she turns away, the light drawing attention to the divots of her collarbones and the feathered curl of her lashes. A single rhinestone flashes from the frayed upturn of her cat's eye. "You wouldn't have to try too hard."

As soon I'm sure she's out of earshot again, I return

my attention to the supine gods: Coyote, true to his nature, is gorging himself on his stack. "Nicely *done*," he says around a full mouth. "Didn't know you had it in you."

"I had a long-term girlfriend for forty-nine years, okay?" Mortality is slippery when Hell doesn't want you. I pick out a strip of bacon with my fingers, the grease still scalding; it's something to do, something to distract the body enough for the mind to prepare for what's coming. I lick the fatty shine from my fingertips, shoot Amanda a look that says *what?* and *please?*

I think I know where this story is going.

I don't want to be right.

"Come on, mami," Coyote purrs. "*Tell* him."

Outside somewhere, Cason is trying to find reception so he can call his kids. Outside, Tanis and Fitz are arguing over the pick-up, seeing if there's anything to scavenge from the banged-up wreck. Outside, a night black as good coffee, air that won't have to hear what I hear. I string bacon into my mouth.

She breathes in. The tendons in her long neck tense against the skin, tremble. "Prophecy is very... *picky* about who is capable of fulfilling its conditions. However, there is some leeway, a kind of failsafe to account for the fact that fate itself is a fractal structure, endlessly expanding into new possibilities with every small decision made. Instead of just requiring a

predetermined roster of names, it calls for—hmm—
actors matching certain criteria, if that makes sense?"

"I'm still following, yeah."

"Okay. *Good*. When Fitz told me about the prophecy,
I ran thousands and thousands of simulations, trying
to figure out the optimal configuration. And when I
was done, there it was. The smoke cleared and you
three were the ones left standing."

I investigate the eggs. The line-chef in the diner's
a virtuoso, wasted in this nowhere truckstop. The
omelette is the perfect French omelette: almost custard
with a glazing of butter, chives and sea salt.

"I know I'm going to hate myself for asking, but
one last question: why us, *specifically?* What's the one
grand attribute that we all share? The thing that pushed
us from mediocre options to great?" My mouth twists
with a bitterness I didn't know I was holding.

"Oh, that's easy," she said. "Of everyone I looked
at, you three are the most willing to die."

COYOTE HOOKS AN arm through the open passenger
window and leans out, his hair twisting loose of its
thick ponytail, the black bleeding away to brindle and
white streaks, like winter's working its fingers through
the mass. He grins, teeth sharp, and sunlight catches
weird in his eyes, turning them gold.

"Did I ever tell you guys the story about how Coyote taught the Internet to read?"

Amanda makes a face. "This didn't happen."

I didn't sleep much the previous night. Amanda's confession wasn't anything that I hadn't already expected, but that didn't change anything: she was right, and somehow, that hurt to know. Fitz and I, we've been wrung dry. Tanis, Cason? It doesn't take a genius to know they'd martyr themselves for the good lives they've made. We're not acceptable damage; we're the frontliners, the vanguard, meat to placate the grinder. Like we've always been, always will be.

"But it did! You don't have to like the truth, Little Sister, but it'll come for you all the same, sure as I'm going to be road kill one day." The radio quiets, Tom Waits gargling a curse as Coyote taps out a beat on the dashboard with a long, lithe hand. The world wraps around the spindle of his song, stills to listen as the demigod lifts his voice, laughing. "That's the problem with you new gods. You hate tradition so much, you won't admit you're just the next generation. Nothing new, just something borrowed."

I glance over to Tanis and Fitz, leaning together, shoulders like steeples, the lamia's head propped on the Chronicler's cheek, both snoring. Cason sits on the other end, trying to take photos of the landscape blurring past. He wants to bring his son here, someday.

Says that Oregon would be good to teach him how to unwrap the minutes into moments, teach him how to get lost in the good of what's left.

His voice wounded itself on the end of that sentence and the light bled out of his eyes, but he rallied, torniqueting himself with stories of vacations past: gibberish about the Grand Canyon, a layover turned into a second honeymoon in Hawaii. Simple stuff, domestic. Talismans of normal to ward against the future.

"*Rupert.*" The way Coyote drags my name out, fills it with vowels, forces a shudder down my spine. "Rupert, did I tell you that story?"

"You can't tell a story that never happened," Amanda hisses, fingers blanching as she grips the steering wheel tighter.

"I taught humanity to write. I stole them fire. I gave them everything, and Zeus gave me eagles to tear out my liver."

"That was Prometheus."

"That was me too." Coyote's tongue lolls out, long and pink, dragging in the wind. "And if you asked Anansi, he'd tell you that he freed the salmon and so on and so forth. Because, what the fuck is the use of a trickster if he isn't writing his own fanfiction?"

"That doesn't even make sense."

"*You* know it makes sense, Rupert. *You* tell 'em."

Suddenly, the backseat floods with the smell of anise and chicory, New Orleans in a cocktail glass. Coyote ashes the cigarillo he hadn't been holding a second ago, his face red-lit by the cherry's glare. "You know what I'm talking about."

I don't, but then I do. The forest spills away into wine-gold ocean, clouds bruised purple and blood where they lap at the horizon, and there are rock formations in the waters, along the petroleum-smooth shore, like giants, like titans, like gods waiting in the blooming dusk. I have my hands pressed against the glass before I know what I'm doing, staring. The Oregon coast is a colder vista than what I'm used to, lonely as the forever highways of America, and I can smell green in the air that frosts in my lungs.

"Archetypes," I say. "They're all archetypes. Interchangeable."

"Set dressing. Conflicts for the hero. Protagonists," Coyote resumes, chortling through his lecture. "Every component of the story is still just that: variables plugged into the latest, greatest performance. We are all here in service of the narrative."

"You mean we're just puppets, then?" Cason's voice tenses with warning. It's like watching a golden retriever go on the offensive, which is funnier in theory than in practice: when teeth sink into your neck, it doesn't matter if they belong to a wolf or a house pet.

Tanis and Fitz keep sleeping, exhausted, snoring in tandem.

"No, no. If I wanted to say you were puppets, I'd have said you were puppets."

The flash of teeth in Amanda's rear-view mirror, and for a second I see Coyote as he is: a collage of bodies and brushstrokes, pebbling the pane of a woman's smooth brown shoulder, frescoed over canvas, reinterpreted by artists and hipsters and soccer moms starved for substance.

"I'm saying we are all interchangeable parts of a story."

"Still not seeing your point." Cason puts down his phone, both hands palsied into fists on his lap.

Coyote laughs. It is a sound that fills the world, has always filled the world, billowed through the empty rooms of creation, engorged them with light. It's a laugh with an appetite for fuckery, for rejiggering fate's compass to always point towards worst-possible-outcome.

"The father gods are as old as the notion of heroes. You cannot write a story without them. But every story has its actors, and every actor can be instructed to do something else." He cocks his head, all coyote now, so little Coyote, save for the worryingly simian curve of a smile that shouldn't fit his face. "You get what I'm saying yet?"

Cason slams upright, ramming his skull into the ceiling, waking Fitz and Tanis in the process. "For fuck's sake! Will it kill you to just be *straight* with us?"

"What the fuck—?" Tanis bolts upright and sideways, away from the Chronicler and into me, causing *my* head to ricochet against the window, before she sinks her face into cupped hands. "This is fucking purgatory. I have sinned and this is my punishment."

I grind the heel of a palm into my temple, wincing. "At least you slept through some of it."

"Koulev—"

"Don't fucking call me that."

"What would Maman say about all this? Sex with her is a holy privilege. There are people out there who would cut you for your disrespect—"

"What are we even talking about?" Fitz yawns, his halitosis physical: a miasma redolent of beef and starch and strangely, the lemonade we'd inhaled six hours ago. Marie wouldn't let us leave until we were glutted on breakfast. She gave me her number then, a note with it: *for when you come back*. I don't know if it was swagger, faith in her fine self, prescience or hope, but I have it in a front pocket, folded like a prayer.

Fitz one-twos me out of my reverie with a coughing fit. "Jesus, open a fucking window. Smells like Christmas died in here."

"Every fucking window in the car is open," I bark

back. "Although I don't know why it matters, we're still on the road to annihilation."

"We're talking about the koulev's sins and how she was tempted by a loa's tit," Coyote purrs. "I bet she hasn't told her sweet Naree yet. You're going to take that little secret to Hell with you, aren't you?"

"Why is this even a topic of discussion? I—" Tanis flicks her tongue over her teeth, chest fluttering with shallow breaths. "I don't understand. This has nothing to do with the mission."

"How are your friends going to trust you if they don't know how deeply you've fucked up? All they see is the mythical beast who ate the heart of a prophet. A good mother. A good *wife*."

"I know you ignored me the first time I asked you questions about this. But seriously, you actually ate someone's heart? Tell me you at least cooked it. With sauce. Heart is drastically overrated as meat, and—"

Fitz reaches around Tanis and with great deliberation, if minimal effect, punches me in the shoulder.

"Shut up. Just shut up."

"Shutting up."

"Look, I'm going to go out on a limb here and say you're trying to motivate us by pitting us against a common enemy—"

"Please. Oh, god. Come on. Not now, Cason."

"—but I don't think that's the right way to go about

it. For one, we've already got something we're allied against: the end of the world. More importantly, I don't think there's a single person in this van who can say they haven't messed up in some way. Especially you, Coyote. Don't think I've *forgotten*."

That *edge* again. Like a claw moving under a sleeve of silk. Looking over at Cason, his face dusk-lit by the dimming sun, I revise my opinion again. He isn't soft. He has *softened*, sure. But that cushion is scaffolded by history, years spent being muscle, and okay, maybe I shouldn't have been so dismissive of someone who cut me out of a crocodile god with a hand-saw.

"There he is. I *missed* you, Case." Coyote laughs again, the sound sinuous. "I thought that version of you was buried with Frank."

"He was. He still is. Why the fuck are you doing this, Coyote?"

"Because I can? Because it's *funny* to see you squirm?" The shadow of something canine, long at the shoulders, longer at the twist-tie limbs, sits in place of Coyote: its eyes smoking, the hind legs bent at right angles that should have broken them, but as I watch, they cross, one over another. "Because it's about tradition, and a man on death row always gets a last meal? Or maybe, because I get bored on road trips and it's something to do. Oh, look. We're here. Turn in that the next stop, darling. There we go."

FIFTEEN

WE MAKE TWO stops.

First, Winchester Bay, which isn't so much a town as a footnote: a thin band of buildings around the mouth of the bay, the docks like bad teeth, jutting into the water. What it lacks in human company, it makes up for in boats. He steers us to a stop next to a dollhouse of a pastel yellow motel, before ushering us to forage for canned food, tackle, fishing lures, camping supplies, sourdough bread, jerky in all flavours, the priciest cheeses we can.

"Why are we doing this?" Fitz hisses.

"I don't know." Amanda shrugs as she comes back inside, a hand on her bulging shoulder bag. "But I sure as hell hope this guy Vining isn't in immediate need of six hundred dollars. Jesus, Coyote."

He grins over a shelf stacked full of pet products, arms laden with cat food.

When we're done in the store, Coyote leads us into a bigger settlement, a town called Reedsport. There's more space than people, but inexplicably, it includes a sprawling skate park. We keep going, spurred on by his promises, the boot straining to contain the provisions, the lock double-knotted with rope. *Yes, it's that good. Yes, it's here. Where else would it be? Didn't you read that article about how they found the best burger somewhere remote? It isn't about Cordon Bleu training, it's about love.*

"Love. Right down to the open vein of it. Everything's about love," he croons. "Or meat."

Coyote makes Amanda pull up in front of a restaurant that, at some point, must have been styled as 'Wild West' before someone trimmed it of frills. The sign, though, keeps its hokey, rustic charm, declaring without embarrassment: *Don's Main Street Family Restaurant*.

"Best French dip in creation," Coyote assures us, slipping out of the car. "I've eaten with kings and

I've drunk champagne from the belly buttons of their queens. But nowhere in time or reality is there a better French dip."

"I won't lie." I glance at the sign on its side, another saloon-style thing: a burger with the words *Main Street* beneath the banner. Close by, a billboard advertising award-winning pies. It's earnest in a way that makes my teeth click. "I'm not feeling much confidence."

But we're shepherded inside regardless. The moment we step through, the patrons—an old couple splitting a meringue pie, a coven of teenagers, some truckers, a family on vacation—fall quiet, staring.

Coyote slinks up to the waitress, already flirting her into submission, his Saint Laurents mysteriously vanished, replaced by corduroy and a fisherman's vest, hiking boots with mismatched laces. Despite his forwardness, none of the scrutiny drifts to him. It's just us.

"You know," Fitz leans closer, "the weird thing is that they don't look like they're about to call the cops."

Tanis strokes a thumb over her Beretta. "They don't smell of anything supernatural either. It's very odd."

From behind us, a voice: "You remind me of my girlfriend, first time she came here. But it isn't anything personal. You're just very clearly out-of-towners, which is its own brand of weird in these parts. Just…

stop standing around, looking like it's the end of the world, and it'll be fine."

"Yeah, that'd be easy to fake," Tanis mumbles.

I pivot on a heel. The man behind me is a sinewy redhead with an aw-shucks, small-town kind of smile, a baseball cap broadcasting allegiance to New York perched astride messy curls, and inexplicably, a hoodie with a Pokéball logo stitched above the heart. "Stop looking so nervous. Anxiety bleeds out."

Advice dispensed, he pads into the restaurant, joining a round-faced Chinese woman in a leather jacket. I almost go over, but Coyote saunters back, his arm around the waitress's waist. His glee is tangible. Finally, someone who respects his magic enough to humour its repercussions.

"We have a table," he declares, grandiose, with all the fanfare of someone announcing a cure to cancer. "Babyface said she got us the best one in the house."

She titters on cue.

They walk off. Fitz goes first, mumbling to himself. I can see now what the redhead meant. It is a tension in the shoulders, a stiffness of the hips, the walk, the way the body points itself towards all available exits, the stop-start of a gait meant to melt into a crowd of thousands. Chameleon tricks, down to the outfit: cargoes, trainers, hoodie, all in dollar-store colours.

I flick a glance at Tanis. Leather jacket, different strut,

but same look. If Fitz hides by looking too ghetto to matter, Tanis achieves the same with the reverse. On her part, the lamia looks excruciatingly like trouble. The Remington probably doesn't help.

Which leaves me.

I look down.

Tattooed Chinese man with a wardrobe of scars.

Not suspicious at all.

"Do we *really* have to stop for that stupid sandwich?" I hiss to Tanis.

She shrugs. "Apparently."

"You said there was a dog on the black road."

"Mm-hm."

"Is it possible that it might be another kind of dog? What if we found a talking German shepherd somewhere? I'm sure that'd work. Maybe a retriever, they know how to fetch. They could fetch the father gods—"

"We have two choices." Another loose-boned shrug. "Have a sandwich with Coyote, or listen to Amanda scream about how much she hates him. You pick."

Then Fitz utters a long hitching croak, eyes wide, and begins clawing at his throat. He chokes out a few sounds that could be syllables before giving up, letting them thin into this reedy endless whine that keep climbing. Higher, higher until it reaches a summit only the castrati visit. Then it happens.

Fitz begins to bleed.

Ears, mouth, nose, eyes. Until the whites are rinded with red and his lashes, wet, stick to the sclera. His jaw cracks open, tongue unrolled. Blood keeps pouring. He mashes his hands into his hair, mute, fish-mouthing for air, and this is the point where Tanis kicks out of her chair, starts howling for medical assistance.

He slumps. I circle around to the other side of the table, wadding up napkins uselessly, hoping I can at least staunch the flow, keep Fitz from bleeding out before an ambulance gets here. The Chronicler is panting now, head buried in his arms, nails digging into his scalp until their beds flush red.

I touch a hand to his shoulder. "Fitz. Jesus, Fitz. It'll be okay. Breathe, breathe, breathe. You don't want to end up in shock. You've got to keep breathing. Calm down."

What I don't expect is his arm lashing out, fingers knotting in my shirt, wrenching me to his face, pulling me close enough to hear what he has been saying all this while, what I thought was the rasp of air. "Heishereheishereishereishere."

His voice breaks off into a sob at the exact instant Amanda explodes through the door. "*Get the fuck out of here—*"

But it's too late.

I forgot that Fitz is a receiver. I forgot that's why

he's a strung-out ex-addict who had decanted decades into anything, *anything* that would give a break from the hallucinations. I forgot this is what happens when there's too much electricity running through a machine: its fuse box pops, it liquefies, it *fries*.

"He's here," Fitz gasps into my shirt, the fabric turning sodden with wet heat.

Coyote sighs, and in his mouth, the name is an invocation and an epithet and a curse and a worship. "*Marduk*."

The blue sky rots black with storm clouds, fog running in ink swirls through the crack in the windows, the open door.

A bell jingles, small and pert, vulgar in its delicacy.

Amanda—pupils in pinpoint, brown irises blown-out, only green left behind—staggers from the Vestibule, brought halfway down to a knee.

"You heard Amanda. We have to get Fitz out of here." Tanis is already crowbarring Fitz into a position that will let her lift him: one shoulder under his armpit, one arm around his waist. "I don't know what is going on, but"—she falters—"it can't be good if someone's bleeding out of every orifice."

"I don't know about *every* orifice—"

"*Don't*."

"There's nowhere to go." Coyote lights a cigarette with a flame at the end of his tongue, head tilted back impossibly, the inside of his mouth gilded with blue shadows until he gulps the light down with a puff of smoke. "Even if you got to the door, you'll just end up inside again. The kings of kings, the gods of the gods, the all-stars; when they make an entrance, they expect you to watch."

The hummadruz registers too late. In the initial panic, I'd ignored it, thinking it tinnitus, some fault of the ears. I've died so many times I no longer expect my cochlea to remember the factory settings. But now, I *hear*.

The patrons, every single one of them, sitting straight-backed in their booths, eyes clouded over, are whispering. Chanting. Their mouths move with near-synchronicity, rictusing into configurations that suggest whoever authored their choreography has no idea how the human mandible operates—or if they did, has no appreciation for the line between functionality and failure. Where the body can be coerced into action while enduring increasing values of pain.

I feel like a cliché, but the words come out. "What are they saying?"

"His names," Fitz moans. "They are speaking his names."

Coyote bobs his head, smoking his cigarette, a kiss deposited into the collarbone of the waitress. She looks—not dead, but something less than alive, shrivelled into a conduit. Chewed-up. Gods subsist on belief; that's why they're in contest over us. But as I stare at the girl, I have wonder if some of them take bigger bites than others.

"He's a motherfucker," Coyote says. "Even for one of his kind. Zeus, he killed his daddy, but in those days, that wasn't anything. But Marduk, though. He ate Ea and Enlil and Eridu and Asaluhi, courted Saparnit with a wedding gift of their gristle. You'd think that was what made him a bastard, but no, it isn't even that. The thing that makes Marduk a right motherfucker, even worse than that murdering Yahweh, is that he told history that it was consensual. That he was their evolution, was given their traits when Babylon became great. But the blood stains are still all over the table cloth."

"Do you ever fucking *shut up?*" Tanis snaps.

And after all that build-up, all that set-work, the cinematography, every mouth in the room keyed to this climactic moment, Marduk's entrance is a spare thing: just a brown hand brushing through reality, as though it were a flap of flayed skin to be waved aside.

Marduk steps into the world with a dancer's grace and a newborn fawn's care, one sandalled foot after another, anklets of gold flashing in the near-light. His clothes do not match: loinskirt, fringed shoulder-cape, a perfectly-pressed dress shirt, the kind that would have set an honest man back a month's wages, *cufflinks*. But he could have been wearing burlap, for all it matters. It's his eyes.

In his eyes are worlds, a ziggurat smoky with prayers and offerings of attar, priests and crowds in praise, every empire laying itself prostrate for him, throat bared and trembling for the heel of Babylon's foot. What else *is* there to do, in the shadow of Marduk, he to whom the gods turned, he who pierced Tiamat's belly, he who made the humans so that they may bear the burden of the divine, he who is supreme, he—?

"You know what, asshole? Fuck your mind tricks. I had enough of this bullshit with my goddamned mother."

Tanis' snarling repudiation of his power snaps it at its neck, breaks the spell enough that I surface, gasping. The lamia thrusts herself between the god and us, tossing Fitz into my arms with a careless motion that reminds me again how strong she is. I totter under the Chronicler's weight, sag into the booth again, head pillowed on my chest. I wrap a protective hand around his skull, fingers sinking into a crusting of hair and blood, and try not to think about how much it reminds me of jello.

Marduk slows, turns, halts at Tanis's posturing, his face rearranging itself to accommodate his displeasure. It is a strange process, peculiarly innocent in the way his features fumble with the idea: that rosebud mouth, so used to magnanimity, jackknifing into a frown; the lineless forehead uncertain of where to crease, the eyebrows at a loss as to how best to express his disappointment.

Tanis raises the Remington, points it at him. A token gesture. There's no conviction in her grip, or in her face, in the set of her shoulders. But she squares her stance, anyway, brings the trigger halfway.

"Get Fitz out of here," she hisses.

"No." Marduk slurs the word, frown deepening, confusion supplanting his disgust at being defied. It hits me, then. He doesn't *understand* language, how trachea and larynx need to cooperate on every sentence. It was burning topiary and omens for him, probably, hallucinations for his priests to origami into commandments. You don't need social skills when you have minions. "Stay."

Everything about him is a little slow, disconnected: the motions and the moods of a god who has to think his way through being human.

"*Fuck* you."

"Not here for you." His eyes roll up and to the right, landing on the trickster. I wonder if Marduk had his meat-suit custom-made, or if he'd commandeered it. "Coyote, we come to speak with you."

Marduk licks his teeth, an obscene sight.

"Go home, dog."

"I didn't know I had a curfew." Coyote drapes his arms across the back of the booth, two fingers on his right hand crooked in a Bruce Lee gesture. "You should come try the French dip. It's good here."

"Insolent."

Another of his capacious grins. "No more than usual."

"We know what you are doing, Coyote."

"And that has stopped me exactly zero times since the dawn of time. At least half of you govern wisdom, or at least that's what you tell me. But you still don't get it. You don't own it. *None* of you own me."

"Yeah, I think this is where we get out. Don't want to be in the way of a family inci—"

Until the day I close my eyes one final time, I will always remember Tanis shooting first. In a quick draw with a god, it was the lamia who won. The blast purees the lower half of Marduk's face and what remains looks like chilli on the verge of done, except here, there: bone fragments, a crescent of teeth, miraculously whole; the tongue, bulbous and lurid, beached in carrion.

"I'll hold him off." And just like that, she's not coming home. She looks over her shoulder, wild-eyed, her grimace desperate. "Tell Naree I'm sorry. Tell Bee—"

She doesn't finish. Amanda's voice floats up like a corpse on a river: *You're the ones most willing to die.* She isn't wrong. Tanis, Cason, they talk a good game about going home, but you know how the story goes. When you become a parent, when you love someone—*really* love them, like it'd break you, like a fish-bone in the back of your mouth, stabbing you every time you swallow—everything else is surfeit. You find out what's extraneous, how love bleeds other sentimentalities away. In that way, it's a parasite, I guess. A nerve agent. Love drives us to madness.

Meanwhile, Marduk, still upright, places his fingertips on the wreckage of his face. His brow furrows, or tries to, sending a knot of ruined tissue swaying. He skewers us with his one remaining eye, the other popped by the blast, and gurgles. Coyote starts laughing so hard the world crimps in his vicinity, the air around him impacted like broken glass, like foil scrunched in a hand: eye-watering, vivid.

Tanis fires again.

Blam.

Brain splatters on the wall behind Marduk, Pollockian. Smoke wisps from the ragged quarter-circle carved into his skull, the bar of his cheekbone swaying like a loose door hinge: a single strip of white bone against the gore. The god blinks. And then he sighs, clearly disgruntled, although it's anyone's guess if he's incensed by the attempt or by its ineffectiveness.

I'm trying to drag Fitz from the commotion when the Chronicler lurches upright, lifts an inch from the tiles and hangs there, as though on an invisible hook. His mouth opens, blood drooling in glossy threads. What issues is his voice, is not his voice, is something like his voice amped up to a thousand, electric like the instant before lightning hits, and his lips do not move, and his tongue is a road of red, and his voice is not his but Marduk's made flesh and tortured gristle.

"We *loved* you."

I shiver, stepping back. "Fitz. Jesus, Fitz…"

"You held your hands to us in the dark and you begged us for light, and we came." Marduk sighs through Fitz's lungs. "We gave you everything, gave you meaning, gave you reason to believe that the night will end. Under our guidance, your kingdoms flourished and mankind became as locusts, your shadow falling on every corner of this earth."

Fitz twitches, a paroxysm that swells in waves until it's too much for his body to hold, and he palsies in place. Still Marduk's voice comes from his mouth, lilting and smoke-rough.

"What do you want, Marduk?" I manage. If there is anything I have learned in all these years, it is that gods like to talk.

"Quiet." The stalk of Marduk's face turns, his attention returning to Coyote.

The trickster's doubled over, an arm around his waist. Still laughing, cheeks wet with tears.

"Come home."

"I ain't going anywhere."

"You are our dog."

"*Coyote*, Marduk!" He unfolds like the wrath of nations brought low for too long, bringing a hand down onto the table hard and making the cutlery jump. Coyote rises, snarling, his human self shivering from his skin, a winter coat shed all at once. What is left behind is an impression, godhood like a bark of gunpowder: raised hackles, jaws that could eat up the whole of creation. "I stole Buffalo's children, I am the one who named the months. I am the one who made death what she is. You *drank* to me in your halls and every one of you called me brother. How *dare* you call me a dog, Marduk! You know better than that."

"And this is why you are not dead," Marduk says evenly, radiant despite his mutilation. "Come to heel and all shall be well. Yahweh did not listen and he is dead, his bones now toothpicks for our table."

I crab-walk across the room without anyone taking notice, Marduk having commanded our silence, but not our stillness. His splattered cerebral matter has begun to run, yoghurt-like, down the wall. I look at my palm, jellied with Fitz's blood. I have a plan and this is, even by my standards, an incredibly dumb idea.

Over Marduk's shoulder, I see Coyote grin, one corner of a mouth that is mostly smoke curving to bare a gleaming tooth.

"You ate Yahweh? Tell you the truth: that doesn't surprise me any. You've probably had an eye on him since the wane of Babylon. How many millennia has it been, Marduk? How long have you dreamt about filleting his haunch, huh? Browning it first. Slow-cooking it with garlic roasted on the fire until its gone that nutty-sweet gold. Thickening it with his blood. I bet you made the first cut, didn't you?"

Patter. That is where the real magic is, forgotten amid the flourishes, the operatic resurrections, the meteorological wonders, the smoke, the glamour, the woman sequined in bright colours, sawed in half as she smiles for the camera. People forget that none of it would exist without the patter, the words that draw the eye from the point where one reality is swapped for another. Coyote keeps babbling and Marduk listens, while Tanis glares daggers at me, Remington tightly gripped. She mouths at me, *What the fuck are you doing?*

I shrug, mouth back, *The hell do I know?*

Truth is, for once: I do know. Sort of. I can see where

it branches from here. There are two choices. One uses Fitz's blood as barter, Marduk's flesh as bait. I open the door inscribed on my arms and I push them both inside, hope one prophet can be substituted for another. That would be the wiser option, which is why I immediately go with option two.

I float a prayer up to Guan Yin, to the small gods of lucky breaks, and press my palm into the wall, three fingers curled, index and thumb splayed out. *Let Marduk have built this body himself, because if he didn't, I will have spent fifteen seconds finger-painting with brains for no reason.*

It is a filthy spell, cheap, quick as an office Christmas party mistake. Blood to bind, blood to bond. It hitchhikes on Marduk's power like a tick, rides it up to the god and opens a valve, turns a one-way transmission into a two-way channel. Looking in from the outside, you wouldn't see anything save for a man doodling hieroglyphs on the wall, occasionally pausing to rub curds of brain between his fingers, which is, in hindsight, what the youth of today might call 'a lot.'

Whatever the case, if I am right, this should stop Marduk dead in his tracks.

I dot the last rune, trying—and failing—not to be disappointed with the sloppiness, the uneven calligraphy. Luckily, infernal forces do not, as a whole, pay much attention to linework. A scream ripples through the restaurant, a scream picked up and amplified by every human mouth in sight, a scream that goes on until there is only this growling, wretched, basal whine, like the lowing of cows in a killing chute. Marduk goes down, chin slamming into the edge of a table, and without any structural integrity, with so much of his face already mush, the rest of it now erupts into pink jelly.

"Jesus on a pogostick, that worked." I blink madly.

Coyote vaults over the table, whooping, human again, catching Fitz one-armed as he collapses. The trickster flings our prophet over his shoulder, beaming. He tips the sharp brim of a pork pie hat at us, while the rest of the details fill themselves in: monochrome hachures, like he's a cartoon character being painted in.

"What the fuck did you—you know what? I'm getting really sick of opening sentences with that." Tanis mashes a hand into her face, already running, her long-legged lope carrying her faster than me by a mile. "Next time, someone tell me what the fuck you're going to do before you do it. Also, what the fuck is up with that—?"

"Father god," Coyote singsongs, grinning. "Weren't you paying attention?"

I throw a look back at Marduk. He is beginning to

rise again, meat sloughing in clumps, bone gleaming underneath. I can see a vertebra tearing through the carnage; an eye opens in the marrow, blue spoked with golden light.

"Good plan, by the way." Coyote keeps going, keeps his patter going, and I'm reminded that it isn't only magicians who subscribe to the church of verbal distractions. Doctors, nurses, combat medics, EMTs, anyone who has had to talk a man away from paying attention to the fact half of him is steamrolled flat. The question is, who exactly is he doing it for? "Gods take bodies when they think they have to talk to their dinner. The father gods, they don't usually need to mess around with that. Pain isn't something they're accustomed to. That must have felt like a *truck*."

A flash of an image: an eighteen-wheeler coming down the tarmac, headlights like twin suns and then pain, supernovaing in fractal patterns, branching across the skeleton, bones splitting, the force of impact so hard that the heart bursts—

I gasp.

—intestines spread across the road, separated by vultures. A dead coyote's grinning face, veiled in little black ants—

"Sorry, reality takes a minute to reset." Coyote shoulders out of the door and the air greets us with a slap, damp and salt-drenched. He licks his teeth. Fitz's blood pearls harmlessly on his outfit like he's wearing plastic. "There we go. Now, where *is* Amanda?"

On cue, the familiar black SUV screams into view, Amanda half-hanging from her window, with Cason in the backseat, holding the door open as the vehicle thunders close.

"What the fuck?" she screams, thumping the wheel for emphasis.

"Is that the designated catch phrase for your group? Do you have a sponsor? Because I can absolutely see that working—"

"Shut. *Up*."

WE ROARED OUT of Reedsport onto the first convenient exit, found ourselves en route to a college town named Corvallis, which Amanda professed to 'not hating.' It is bigger than Reedsport, built to accommodate itinerant parents. There would be motels. Places to stop, regroup, rethink our strategy—maybe even formulate one, to actually revise.

"How's Fitz?" Amanda tenses her grip on the wheel, knuckles blanched of colour.

"He has been worse," I say.

There's a pause, a silence too big to be absorbed without awkwardness. Then, Cason says, "It could have been herpes."

The backseat is a thin soup of blood, shallow puddles collecting in the ridged leather. Cason and I spend twenty minutes drenching Fitz in mineral water, rinsing him as best we can. Every capillary in his eyes burst during the ordeal, and the blood is beginning to coagulate, darkening the sclera. But there is no other indication of damage. He is breathing, at least.

"Should we get him to a doctor?" Amanda asks.

Coyote reaches around from the passenger seat and wafts a nonchalant hand over Fitz's face. "He'll be alright. You people never read the Bible? It was all in fashion back then. Making prophets wander the desert for decades, making them walk until they bleed. They're resilient. They always bounce back."

"Since when were you such a good Christian boy, Coyote?" Tanis snarls from the seat behind me, shotgun between her knees, cheek rested on the barrel.

"I'm not." He laughs gauzily. "I was just askin' if you'd read it."

I rummage through the jumbled memory of our encounter with Marduk, draining another bottle of cold mineral water over Fitz's face. He doesn't stir. With the edge of my shirt, I begin dabbing again at the blood scabbing in his nostrils. "Can you heal him?"

"Who's to say that I haven't done so already? With that pass of my hand, I may have put him into a healing sleep, and sent him on his path—"

I don't point out that Fitz was already comatose.

"I think Rupert was talking something more instantaneous." The sneer comes through in Tanis's low, hungry rasp. "Something befitting a father god."

Coyote grinned. "You're not that much of a disappointment after all, koulev. I'm beginning to see what Maman Brigitte saw in you, although I think I like them less in love with murder—"

I cut in. "So she's right? You *are* a father god."

"Father god-*adjunct,* maybe. I've been called a demiurge a few times, and that feels more correct. I don't have a pantheon. I just have peers. When we get together, worlds don't come to be, but sometimes there's a party and sometimes, that spills into a *story*—"

Tanis lets out a hiss. "That's why it was you who had to lead us to the black road."

"To be fair, you could have probably used Raven or Bunny instead, although I think you'd have trouble with the latter." A flash of his teeth in the rearview mirror.

"You could have told us." Cason finally speaks up, betrayal hemming a voice otherwise dulled to grey. He strips Fitz of his socks, face contorting at the stink of four-day feet, and replaces them with a fresh pair. "You could have told us."

"No one asked." The answer is reproachful but

bright. "You took the koulev's prophecies at face value, and came looking for a dog who could lead you to a black road. None of you thought to ask why that dog and not the other, and how a *dog* could do such a thing—"

The stress he puts on the word *dog*, it feels like he's tugging on something, drawing it up tight and away from public scrutiny. Coyote is angry: a brittle, sugar-glass emotion, like the veneer that is starting to break.

The woods become fields, far as forever, dark honey in the storm-light. In the distance, I see wind turbines: futuristic contraptions, colossal, sleek-bodied silver.

"Amanda, did you know?"

She doesn't answer, keeps driving.

"What I said earlier, it still stands." Coyote winds down a window and lights up another cigarillo. This one smells like ozone, like lightning at the point of contact. "Whatever my parentage, I will still lead you to the black road."

"Even if it means you dying," Tanis says.

"Koulev, you saw what happened at Don's restaurant. Let's say that I wanted to two-time you. Wouldn't I have done it yet?"

"Could be a ruse," Tanis grumbles tiredly. "Could be a long con."

"I promise you there's nothing better than instant gratification."

"Is Fitz going to be alright?" Cason whispers.

"I wasn't lying about the healing sleep. He dreams of prairies and endless forests and nights unsoiled by electric lights. When he wakes, he will be fine." Coyote's voice gentles as he takes a drag, the cherry burning green this time. "As for dying, it isn't so bad. Ask Rupert. Death is—"

"A terrible motherfucking thing to endure. Why would you even attempt to romanticise it, you sick asshole?"

"Because that is why we tell stories, Rupert. To make ourselves feel better about what we cannot change. Like you, I could have chosen to not be part of this. But love—" Coyote chuckles bleakly. "It makes us fools. Now, let's find a motel so we can wait until the prophet rises."

"As long as there are no more crocodiles."

"Shut up, Rupert."

SIXTEEN

I SLIDE ONTO the bar stool and sag, fingers wrapped around a glass of cheap bourbon. Sleeping hasn't been easy; I didn't even try this time. Luckily for me, Corvallis keeps collegiate hours and collegiate prices, meaning the bars cost nothing if you don't mind mainlining sweetened mouthwash.

I probably could have chosen someplace less *sticky*, though.

"This seat taken?" Coyote's voice, sanded down to something human, comes over my shoulder as I dip my fingers into the glass of cold water I'd ordered with my alcohol, rubbing the grime off against an ice cube.

"No. You can sit, if you want." I raise my head. Tonight, he looks about eighteen and unsure of himself, the hoodie too big on shoulders that'll still take a few years to fill. He's still handsome, of course—gods can't abide by poor aesthetics—but at least he's trying to come down to my level. I can appreciate that. "Would you care if I said 'yes'? Is anything *ever* sacred to you?"

"Yes." He sits down. The moment his elbow makes contact with the bar, there's a glass in his hand like it's always been there, the contents an expensive shade of pale leather. The strobing lights from the bar's one disco ball turns the ice inside opalescent. "More than a few things. Questions are sacred."

I sip my scotch and say nothing.

"Hope. That is holy to me too." He tents his fingers around his glass and stares at the rows of cheap booze behind the bar. "Pity that there is so little of that these days. Your kind has become so tired of being alive."

"Can you blame us? World is ending. In more ways than one." To our right, a crowd of twentysomethings roar over a game of beer pong, the contestants like gladiators glorying in the exaltations of the mob. "There's nothing to do but count the hours until closing time."

"No. But you know that is the manna that sustains the new gods, right? That ennui. Humanity only believes in distractions these days."

"You know, you can't keep blaming secularism for all your ills."

"Oh, I don't. Some of the others might, but I don't. Everything dies, Rupert. No grift is perfect. Nothing survives forever; that's what tricksters have been trying to teach mankind since you first could speak. But you keep hoping it's a bad joke, that you'll keep going, that tomorrow will be here, that you can defer everything that makes you afraid because there are always more days to come, rolling on like the highways of an American folk song." He downs his drink. When he brings the glass down with a solid thump, it is full again, two fingers of aged gold. "But there aren't. Not even for gods."

"Aren't you afraid?"

"Terrified. But that's what makes these last days so good, Rupert. I know these are the only ones I have left." He bares his teeth at me. "What're you drinking?"

"Southern Comfort. Tastes like a diabetic's piss." I sip more of it, anyway.

"*Why* are you drinking, it then?"

Two girls stumble together so the back of one is pressed against the bar, the other molding herself to her, and they kiss like they could eat each other whole, while the milling boys howl encouragement.

"Because I'm taking handouts from the Internet." I shrug at him. At this point in the night, I'm out of pretences. "You know, it isn't really easy to build up a nest egg in my situation. Even harder, when you're unemployed with a criminal record."

"Caol Ila." The girls separate, laughing, giddy with what could be their sixth Long Island or the first shiver of true love. There's applause. Their eyes glide over us, across me like I'm invisible, but one of them—her hair in a 1920s flapper bob, so thin I can see the spokes of her joints through her tanned skin—pauses to rest two fingers on Coyote's arm, as though to ask or accord a benediction.

"Excuse you."

"Every man needs a signature beverage, Rupert. Something that defines him. If you're English, it's easy: a gin and tonic, *properly* prepared. French? You whisper to the bartender each time a name that sounds like sex. Wine red as blood and old enough to love." He glances over, teases his hand under her fingers and kisses the ridge of her knuckles. Blushing, the girl retreats with her new lover, tumbling into the crowd.

"I don't see how any of that is relevant—"

"It isn't." He smiles at me with uncharacteristic shyness, a rawness in his expression that hurts somehow to see. I wonder for a minute if Coyote had ever been young, if gods come out full-grown, screaming scriptures at the earth, or if for a little while, he lay silent, staring at the primordial sky, breathless with wonder at what was to come. "But I wanted to leave you with something when I'm gone, a blessing. I don't give those out very often. "

He spins to face me, a hand closing over the brim of my glass. I recoil from the intrusion. "What. Are. You. *Doing?*"

"From now until the day you die, your cup will never be parched. There will—"

"Wait."

"—always be Caol Ila in your glass, the finest in ten miles, and you will never be lonely of the best whisky the Isle of Islay may offer." He twirls his hand up with a flourish, beaming, every tooth on parade.

I look down at my glass, appalled, the watered-down remains of my drink replaced by a spirit that reeks of antiseptic, of simmering peat moss and—bizarrely—of smoked ham. "I didn't even say I liked scotch."

"It's a drink befitting heroes. You'll learn to appreciate it." He sniffs. "Besides, gifts are better when they're something you grow into."

"I take back every kind thing I ever made the mistake of saying to you. Also, what if I want water? Or orange juice?"

"Keep a mug close by. Or a water bottle, or a saucer, or anything that isn't glass. At any rate, I think you will be grateful later."

Coyote flags down the bartender, a stout boy of mixed parentage, his curly hair cropped close to a good-looking face only slightly marred by a cauliflower nose slowly coming back from whatever had broken it, one cheekbone plum-black from likely the same encounter. "Buffalo wings, if you have them. With blue cheese sauce."

"We have the buffalo wings," says the bartender, drying a glass. "But I'm afraid we don't have any blue cheese sauce. Or blue cheese, for that matter."

"But you have cheese," Coyote says. "Melt whatever you have into a dipping bowl for me. Ooh, and bring some ranch, too."

"You're not really big on checking in with other people, are you?"

He shrugs. "In the old days, depending on where you met me, there would have been a real feast. Venison, wild greens fried in duck fat, bison ribs, berries like you couldn't imagine, salmon roasted just so with nothing but a bit of salt and lemon. Perfect as going home."

He shakes his head solemnly. "We would have eaten like kings," he says. "Now, you get buffalo wings."

"Dinners can't be choosers."

"What?"

"Sorry. Just thinking aloud." I take an experimental swallow of the Caol Ila. It's better than the initial whiff suggested. Oaken, with undernotes of toffee and a seaside aftertaste, a tang of brine far less foul than I'd worried it would be.

"Tomorrow, we go back to Winchester Bay. The black road that Tanis saw, it has a beginning there in the dunes for which that place is famous for." Coyote toasts me, grandiloquent even in that single gesture. Again, his expression falters, becomes boyish in fluttering, thick-lashed embarrassment. "When I am gone, be sure to raise a glass to me from time to time. It will be nice to be remembered."

I drain my glass and place it back down. True to Coyote's word, it is full again. Two fingers of amber liquid, with a single frosted ice cube sweating inside. "Aren't you already flushed with worship? Every hippie in San Francisco is tattooed with your face. You're in all the stories—"

"There's a book I like a lot, one written by an Englishman, and made into television by some Americans. In it, there's a chapter where one god tells another that though her feast-days are celebrated, although people still drink and eat to her name, not a soul remembers where the tradition comes from. It's like that with me, Rupert." His voice drops, so quiet I can barely hear him over the electro-pop. "But worse. So much worse. When my bones have been gnawed to the marrow, and they're wearing my name like a cheap costume on Halloween, I'd like to know one mortal still remembers the whole of me."

"That's a lot of responsibility for someone you have recently declared would die really soon."

"Pff. You're like a disease, you'll always find a way to come back."

"Probably sounded more flattering in your head."

"I enjoy your confidence in the regard of others." His smile is a grotesque half-moon. "Not that that's the point, but I have my reasons."

"Wouldn't Cason be a better candidate for this? I mean, the grandson of the *Devil*. That is impressive pedigree."

Coyote fixes me with a cool incredulous stare. "Has anyone told you that you talk entirely too much?"

"Cason thinks it's a natural consequence of excessive amounts of trauma. Humour as a means of self-control." I hesitate, feeling more is needed. "You know."

"Fascinating."

The buffalo wings arrive now, on an altar of celery sticks.

"Yet somehow," he continues, examining the dip with a hint of disdain, "you didn't answer the question."

Exhaustion prickles under my skin like pinfeathers. "Yes. More times than you can imagine."

"Believe it or not, I can imagine *exactly* how often you've been told to shut up, and more." Coyote fishes a wing up by its breaded end, tips his head back and lowers it into his mouth. One eye on me, he bites down, crunches through bone and gristle like they were both as succulent as a newborn hare. "Now, eat. Tomorrow, we both die."

COYOTE WAKES US at sunrise, every lock falling open at his hollering, the sky pink as the inside of a mouth and a hangover like a cancer behind my right eye.

"Asshole."

My first glimpse of the world is his face, leaning over mine: pink tongue, teeth and canine halitosis panted straight into my nostrils. Strings of warm saliva sink gracefully onto my face. Without thinking, I reach up and shove at his muzzle, flinging Coyote aside. He cackles into the gloom, vaulting from my bed onto Cason's, front paws coming down on the man's chest with a pop of cartilage. I wince sympathetically.

"Wake up!"

"Jesus fucking—"

"—Magdalena?" Coyote inquires with a wag of his tail. "What a filthy little family you belong to."

I fumble onto my side to peer blearily at the clock on the nightstand. It reads five-thirty am, which is just about what I'd expect, given the tines of rosy light stretching across the the blinds. Digging the heel of a palm into one eye, I sit up. Note to the wise, to the health conscious, the ones who rightfully worry about cirrhosis in their old age: don't go drinking with gods. Least of all tricksters drunk on their coming deaths.

Coyote nips, snarls, bites, tugs, barks with the gusto of a border collie, shepherding us along morning ablutions with manic enthusiasm. He scrabbles at the bathroom door while Cason shaves, howling, "The black road will wait for no one!"

"This is why I wanted my own goddamned room." Cason bangs on the door three times in reply, and Coyote laughs, doubling over onto the floor, before he dives out our door.

At last we're done, shambling out of our rooms, groaning. Even Amanda looks beleaguered, more human by the day, more battered by the ongoing production that is being alive. I pass her a styrofoam cup of bad coffee.

"The black door won't wait. Come on, come *on*." Coyote bounds up to our van, blurring between species, the brindled coat and paintbrush tail hung up for Saint Laurents, a grey silk tie, brogues like black oil. "Today is an excellent day to die."

No one speaks on the drive back to Winchester Bay except for Coyote, undulating between languages, wefting creation myths with cataclysmic data about the world's destruction, numbers in kaleidoscope, until there's no end or beginning, no chronology. The world smells implausibly of scotch forgotten on a cold windowsill: peat, pear, caramel, smoke, fresh snow.

Then, quicker than any of us might have liked, we're there.

"Aren't they beautiful? When the wind stirs them, even humans can sometimes see beyond the worlds here." Coyote plants fists on his hips, legs spread, a prideful look to his face. As though he made this, as though the flexures of golden-white sand belong to him. "They don't like talking about it, but every year, people vanish into the dunes."

His grin is enormous. "Their bones are the sweetest."

"Have you ever wondered what would happen if we weren't a part of this mess? Like, where you would be?" Fitz comes up beside me, hair shaved so close I can see the colour of his scalp beneath the down.

"Eating noodles and watching a football match," I reply immediately, then regret the glibness. The thought of food has me nauseous. "How you doing?"

"I don't know. I think—I think I can hear them. But they're not here, I don't think." His shoulders droop. "I don't know if that matters either. Marduk isn't dead. They know we're coming." He pauses. "For what it's worth, I'm sorry."

My attention drifts to where Amanda is picking up an argument with Coyote, their voices low, too low to permit eavesdropping, but whatever's happening, it amuses the trickster no end, and terrifies the younger goddess, her complexion bleaching. Her gestures are quick, angry.

"What for?"

"The fact that you're here." Fitz huddles into himself, shoulders drawn up, hands thrust deep into pockets. "That we're all here. That this is happening. That it's happening to *you*."

My blood curdles into something cold and my tongue goes thick. Hard to tell whether it's dread or the hangover. "Coyote's right, isn't he?"

"Prophecy isn't a precise science." The automatic defence. "It might not happen."

"But you saw it."

"I saw *something*. I don't know if it'll come to pass. Not everything does. Fate is subjective, and—" He sucks air through clenched teeth, as though stung by the next words. "You're our friend. We won't let anything happen to you."

"I don't think we have a choice."

Coyote peels from his conversation with Amanda and is waving us forward, bouncing on his heels, a kid on the borders of Disneyland. I turn from Fitz to walk towards the dunes, sunlight flattening the dunes, stealing their dimensionality, so they're nothing but white.

"I don't think we ever did."

When we've all gathered in front of him, Coyote bows extravagantly like a circus ringmaster, all pomp and pageantry, one arm poised beneath his ribs, the other flung out, one leg thrust behind him in a near-curtsey.

Amanda glares at him. "You're going to need to stay alert. From what Coyote tells me, this will take you straight to the father gods. I won't be able to help you here but the moment that you're out, I'll"—blood oozes from a nostril, and she wipes it away with the back of a sleeve—"be on the other side. I already have clones waiting in Iceland—"

"Iceland." An incredulous noise from Tanis. "That is a *long* way from here."

"Apparently that's where the father gods go, when they gather." Amanda narrows her eyes at Coyote, who smiles primly, hands folded at his belly. "So he tells me."

"So the road shows."

"If I don't make it back," Cason begins, who'd not said anything since we arrived in the dunes, the breeze tugging at a few strands of hair from its helmet of pomade. He is dressed better than he ever has been. Sunday clothes.

Or a dead man's last suit.

He tries again. "If I don't make it back, that clone thing—can you make a copy of me too? Someone needs to update the will. Make sure that the mortgage is order, check on the college funds. There are a lot of things."

His voice shrinks through the list until it's a rasp, breath sawing through teeth, slow, too slow, like if he tries anything else, he'd break.

"I'll take care of everything. For as long as I can," Amanda says, after a long while. "If something happens, none of your families will be left wanting."

"Okay," says Cason.

Tanis exhales, a jagged sound, every muscle in her jaw tight. "Thank you."

And then Coyote tilts his head back, and the black road unwinds from his mouth like he'd swallowed it for a parlour trick. The colour brings to mind something I'd read a few years ago over the shoulder of a man in a carmine suit: an article about a building in South Korea rinded with a nanomaterial that eats the light. It created a 'schism in space,' it said, made the eye see black because we cannot process any way else.

The black road is like that, only it doesn't just fuck with your neuroreceptors but reality as well, shearing through physics, through the spatiality of the world, so that jet-black ribbon, which had looked so small, sprawls now across the dunes. The trees melt from view, swallowed by sand. Coyote lays himself down as the black road continues its metamorphosis, a well-dressed corpse on the lightless tarmac, eyes staring up at nothing, a smile at the turn of his lips. Then, without warning, he is swallowed by the umbral path he's thrown up.

"Whoah," Fitz whispers.

"I know. I like that trick." Coyote's voice from behind us, causing every one of us to jump. "And before anyone starts getting on my case, saying I could have said something about it, no one ever asked me about *my* interpreta—*glurk*."

You'd think that the death of a god would be beautiful. Epic, even. A tragedy as rooted in drama as the male gender's frequent and ill-advised impulse to court post-matrimonial threesomes. Prometheus defined the template: his body yoked to a rock, his liver a perpetually replenishing amuse-bouche for a crèche of immortal eagles. Gruesome imagery, sure, but striking. As the demise of a deity should be.

But Coyote doesn't die like that.

If I hadn't had reason to hate them before, I loathe them now. The father gods, how they'd pulled that cartoon noise of Coyote as he flinches inwards, like he'd taken a blow to his belly, so undignified, so unlike anything the trickster would have allowed himself to say even on his worst days. There's pain in his eyes. He raises his gaze, looks behind our shoulders. We turn as a group, and even if we were blind, we'd have known they were there—Marduk, once again whole, standing abreast with silhouettes like the afterimage of flash bomb—the air full of their power, like steel wool on the tongue.

Marduk brings his hand down like he's Moses halving the Red Sea and Coyote's breastbone cleaves in two. There is no crack, no snap of bones breaking, but we hear instead how intestines unwind: slowly at first, with a distinctive greasiness, slick tubing gliding over itself, then with great urgency, the oiliness suddenly so much more pronounced, as gravity tugs and tugs, until a knuckle-sized button of grey meat exposes itself between two shirt buttons.

His shirt swells with entrails until the weight of them undoes the fabric from the clinch of his belt, and they splatter, steaming, over polished brogues, liver and yards of intestine, more heft to them than you'd think from looking at their gelatine shine. But there you go, there you go.

"Messy," chirps one of them, face a halo of radioactive light. The headdress and the raptorial beak give him away.

Marduk twitches a shoulder indifferently.

"Ra," Fitz whispers, pained, already beginning to bleed again.

The demiurges watch without interest as Coyote crumples onto his side, one arm flung out, the other curled, as though to his entrails were children to shelter in an embrace. A foot twitches. His trousers stain with a growing bloom of shadow, the sudden ammonia in the air shocking not because it is present, but because it has been allowed to exist. The death of a god is supposed to be beautiful.

All at once, I'm furious. That they couldn't conceive a way to spare him the humiliation of dying like roadkill. That he is there. Without his patter, his grace, his protean wardrobe, his conman charm. The road runs long and black behind his executioners, flecked with diamonds.

"Go home," Marduk flutes. "See what was wrought when one would not listen to us. He was told to heel, but he did not."

"The fuck are you doing, talking like a bunch of Ren-faire assholes?" I don't realize until the words are out that I'm the one screaming, that I'm already moving, that there's nothing on me but rage, nothing but a vision of a coyote with his head smashed open, wearing a veil of little black ants like he was wedded to death at last.

None of it matters.

I barrel down on the lords of creation, the highest of high, the sovereigns of their pantheons, the patron gods of dead cities once great, ululating at a falsetto that would have cracked glass, and I swear—just a fraction of a moment, the heartbeat before cartilage snaps—that I see them flinch.

Then, that ceases to matter too.

Wires lasso my wrists, my knees, my ankles, the flesh between my fingers, every joint on my body, no matter how inconsequential. Even my jaw, threading through the insides of my mouth so my tongue can bleed. I have a second to breathe before they raise me into the air, spread-eagled for their inspection, my restraints constricting as the gods drift closer.

"Fucking *hell*, Rupert, do you ever think—?" Tanis snaps from somewhere behind me. My bonds tighten further, slice deeper, my pulse a hundred hummingbirds embedded in my skin.

"No," I manage to wheeze. "Never."

Ra motions with a hand.

The barrier comes up so close to the back of my head that I can feel my scalp bubble, smell the acrid reek as my hair cooks. The flesh peels along the nape of my neck and I scream. I still can hear Tanis, still can hear Fitz, but their voices are distorted by whatever it is that Ra has conjured. I'm alone with the father gods.

This is *definitely* going to end well.

"Noisy," the bird-god says.

Slowly, I begin to discern shapes within that unending glare: close-cut curls and lush beards on aquiline faces, togas; a glass eye set within a wise mien; antlers, rising from a fur-shrouded thing that'd be double my height if we stood toe to toe.

"Hey, *hey*." I kick a foot feebly for attention. "Is this where you do the exposition thing?"

Surprise and syrupy curiosity prickles through the group.

"You know what I'm talking about, right? That's how this works. You capture the opposition and then you tell them your whole plan, down to all the little details. Because otherwise, what's the point? You need someone to show off to, to show you're the smartest dog in the room."

They exchange looks. I'm entranced by their eyes. There's something bovine about those limpid stares, and not only because there are no whites, no sclera, nothing but cozy darkness, like winter nights outside a log cabin.

"No," Marduk says.

And I die.

IN THE BEGINNING of this memoir, I said it happened twenty-six times.

I wasn't lying.

I didn't say how, though.

Once was to a crocodile god bloated with larvae divinity, its insides eaten away until it lay hollow like a cicada shell, marionnetted by its parasites.

The other twenty-five times, it was to these assholes.

SEVENTEEN

I COUNT EVERY death.

You know what they say about the first time? How it's always the hardest? Maybe that's the crux of the old Biblical story, where murder came to be because a man named Caine killed his brother Abel. After that first infraction, humanity becomes proficient at every gradient of slaughter you could pin a name to, whether fratricide or first-degree selfishness, stabbing or drowning or death by drunken blowjob.

I guess it's true for gods too.

The first time they kill me, it's without preamble. My restraints became garrottes, compressing until they cut clean through each joint: phalanges, knees, ankles, wrists, pelvis, individual vertebrae. That I fall to pieces onto the asphalt like so many slices of cured meats is irrelevant; it is a stunningly efficient execution. If I wasn't so busy dying, my decapitated head turning to receive the rain of effluvia, I'd offer compliments to the murderer.

Ordinarily, I'd then segue into processing into Diyu, where I'm reprimanded and reminded of my duties, before resurrection into the same shell.

Not this time.

Instead, I wink back into being, whole and in view of the father gods, who are, I think, as mystified by my restoration as I am. I stare at them, apologetic.

"This doesn't normally happen."

They confer in a tongue like the itching of the lizard brain, a primordial dialect. Then Odin comes up to bat. This second time round, I guess the gods have become curious. From the All-Father, I would have expected incineration, to be rendered down into so much charcoal, but I die perforated by corvids, his ravens too big to peck out my eyes so they just jackhammer my skull to rubble.

Another flash. Another Rupert, ostensibly whole but exponentially more traumatised.

"What the fuck?"

My third death. *Now* they choose fire.

For my fourth, a low-grade electrocution that leaves my organs just so. I die as they pry open the lid of my belly, steam wafting upwards, salt and that distinctive barbecued sweetness.

For the fifth, it's lions. They're traditionalists.

It keeps going.

I want to say it gets easier, but with every iteration, the gods become more inventive, stretching their toolset. The lions become maggots, become rats, become locusts kept starved for millenia. The torments stretch. I became their Vitruvian man and the gods are children, delighting in the puzzlebox of my longevity, adapting from one death to the next. On one occasion, they make it last for a decade. On the next, I detonate, a firework demise so exquisitely agonizing I wake up still choking.

Twenty-five times, until at last something takes pity and the lights don't come back on.

I WAKE TO Meng Po's face, staring upside-down at mine, her dark eyes brimming with worry.

"What have you *done* to yourself?"

I try to sit up, but it doesn't work. Pain strobes across the length of my prone body, tracing the topography of the gods' experimentation, where they broke, where they cut, where they scooped out marrow to taste. "I am offended that you'd suggest it's *my* fault."

"It is usually your fault, Rupert."

"I still feel like it's an unjust critique."

She sighs. "Enough."

The ceiling is raftered with strings of dried herbs, a few ropes of sausage; a domestic inventory, unlike what you'd expect of a divine abode. "Am I dead for good?"

"If you wish to be, yes. There is only so much damage that the soul is allowed before it comes apart."

"What if I don't wish to be?"

"Then I would send you back." Her voice is even, her expression guarded.

"And let's say, let's just say, that there is a pack of gods waiting for me on the other side, and a group of friends—" I pause, repeat the words, let the reverb settle in my head. *Friends*. Who would have thought? "Friends they might kill, if nothing is done. Because frankly, I have no idea what *can* be done. What would you advise?"

"To remember that we are each of us doors and every god is tethered to the fates as much as you and any other mortal." Meng Po ladles tea into a small saucer, lowers it to where my head lies on her lap.

"And more than anything else, it's the ones in power who are afraid."

"I want to point out that I just had the fantastic fortune of dying"—I pause to enumerate my deaths; personal distance is invaluable in these situations—"twenty-four, twenty-five times? I don't know if the rats count; it was the same method twice."

"You're babbling."

With effort, I heave myself upright again. The room is small and spare as a nun's boudoir which, upon reflection, isn't an inaccurate description. To my surprise, it's not Diyu outside of her windows but something more pastoral: meadows and mountains that remind me of the Rockies, snow coroneting their spires. A family of plump bunnies explore the grass.

I sip the tea. "I think I'm allowed."

Meng Po shrugs a delicate shoulder. A vase of fresh flowers—extinct blossoms, I imagine, dead for a thousand years and forgotten save for an ox-headed demon in love with the saint of new starts—sits on a well-worn table.

"I'm not saying you're not." She sips primly from her own cup.

"I still don't understand what you're trying to tell me, though."

"I occasionally wonder if you're intentionally obtuse or just *stupid*." Meng Po says it without rancour, quietly pensive. "Rupert, you've spent your whole life looking for short cuts, cheats, backstage passes, if you will."

"You're hipper than you look."

Meng Po shakes her head carefully. "Pay attention."

"I'm paying attention. I think. This is about as close to 'attention' as I ever get. The father gods, there's no way to kill them—"

"No," says Meng Po. "But that does not mean they are without fears."

"What the hell would people like that be afraid of?" I drain my tea, abruptly furious; every nerve feels like a guitar string stretched too tight. I'm not angry for me; I'm angry for everyone who has been born, who has had to live—knowing or unknowing—through the petty games of the divine, who has been a chess piece: a pawn, a knight sworn to a lord with no love for anyone but his next distraction. What is this world, that it has a God of Missing People *and* a God of Being Missing? What is the *point* of the pantheons if we're all just dying here?

Okay, so I am angry for me too. But that's beside the point.

"What could *gods* be afraid of? Father gods. They're the fucking foundations of heaven. They fucking shit out creation. There's nothing we can do, *nothing* we can do—"

The saucer shatters in my hand. Porcelain shrapnel cuts new lines through my palm, marking out new fortunes. I clench my fingers around the shards but there is no pain, Meng Po's tea is smoky in my mouth. No blood either. Not a drop. I open my hand again to stare at the scored, torn skin. No blood at all; nothing but a strange effervescence, like the ghost of champagne weeping over the dermis.

"—except die. Over and over and over again. As many times as it suits their damned pleasure." My voice dries away. "What the fuck do *we* have that we can use against them? We're just meat."

"And what do you think they fear more than anything else, Rupert? What punishment do they give their own?"

"You're a terrible goddamned quest giver, Meng Po."

To my vicious delight, her expression finally splinters. Her brow creases, the corners of her mouth wrinkle as her lips pinch. "Humour me."

"Okay. Fine. Let's see." I gaze out of the window again. The sky, on second examination, is wrong: wine-dark between the saccading of my eyes, the sun like a hole gouged through the strange fabric. "Let's see. Okay, so there are stories of Zeus turning Apollo into a mortal because he pissed off his old man. And Zhu Bajie, and what's the other one's name—?"

The switch flips.

"Oh," I say. "Oh. Are you saying what I think you're saying?"

Meng Po stares placidly at me. "What do you think I'm saying?"

"I think you're—you know what? Never mind. We're not doing that. I can control myself." I point at her. "I think you're telling me that they're afraid of being meat. Is that right? Is that the big secret that they've been hiding? But that's so stupid."

The goddess shrugs delicately.

"Imagine being immortal—"

"I know what being immortal is like. It's fucking terrible."

"No, not how you understand it. That isn't immortality. That is a function of office and a cruelty that no one deserves."

"You know I'm still in the same room, right?"

"Being a god, Rupert, means knowing with *certainty* that there will be a tomorrow, that the future will be sweet with pleasures, that those pleasures are limited only by the span of your imagination, and that all this will be true… up till the end." Meng Po takes my hand in hers, cool and smooth as ceramic. With care, she picks my palm clean of crockery and closes her fist around the detritus. When she spreads her fingers, there's the saucer again, whole and clean. She nods to herself and pours us both a fresh serving of tea. "That is the big secret. All gods know, without question, that there is an end to paradise, that Ragnarök always comes, that the end times are inescapable."

I trap my hand around the proffered crockery, gleaming with that strange effervescence that oozed from me when I should have bled. "Great. So, they know we can't beat them."

"There are no guarantees in this world, Rupert. You of all people should know that. No promises, no certainties, no signature that cannot be forged, no document that cannot be altered. It is all *lies*." Her fingers close around her own cup and she lifts it to her lips, staring at me over the rim. "Imagine spending an eternity with that knowledge. It can make some people so afraid."

"So, you want us to kill them. I mean, that isn't bad advice, but at the same time, it isn't *useful* advice. The problem is actually getting there. Killing a father god is tough business. Just because they're *going* to die—"

"Time is space," Meng Po interrupts, a smile blooming.

"Are you high? Just tell me what you want us to do. Like, within the context of the prophecy or whatever. There's the Road, the Lamp, the Knife, the Door, the Noun. Explain this to me like it's a video game walkthrough." I puff out my cheeks and sigh, my hands shaking so hard I have to put the cup down. "Just... tell me what to do."

"What's a door sometimes, but the means to join two places?"

"Can we just stop with the—" The light flicks on. "Oh. Really? It's that easy? Just like that?"

I don't hear Meng Po's answer, only see the old woman's shoulders shake with laughter, her head thrown back, teeth gleaming white in that false sunlight. I feel the pull of the father gods, a fishhook sunk deep—but this time, I'm not scared.

"HEY, MOTHERFUCKERS."

I wake up, already flayed: butterflied, skin petalled and pinned to the wall. The pain spasms my belly, spreads in bright wailing colours through my vision. I stare through the flowers of pain, out and over the heads of the father gods. Once again, the scenery feels improbably alien: a desert cauled in ice and extraterrestrial terrain.

"*Hey.*" They've done something to my entrails. Gravity hasn't yet made a pool of them at my feet. "Motherfuckers. I'm talking to you."

"Still noisy," chirrups Ra.

"It's called a conversation." There's an unexpected benefit to unspeakable pain becoming the status quo.

The sensation never goes away, but the body learns to acclimatise, allowing for speech and last-ditch bravado. I clench my teeth, all the while thinking, *We did this before, sixteen deaths ago.* "Interaction, give and take, like equals. You ever heard of that, asshole?"

The plumage around Ra's throat tufts and swells. "Noisy."

"A god cannot be equal to a worm," rumbles Odin. You'd think he'd look good, that one. What with the worship of the big screen, the endless rehashing of his myth, the neo-vikings tweeting for his blessings. But this Odin, he's the God of Gallows, the Hanged One: a sun-dried cyclopean corpse, draped in leathers, antlered and stinking of shadow. "A god is no equal of worms."

I remember Marduk. The father gods, for all their antediluvian power, the largesse of their status, are so divorced from the world they can barely speak its languages anymore. No wonder they fled. They're old men shouting down from a sky once unknowable and now mapped by a thousand thousand data points. No safe place for them anymore, not with secularism giving a name to every miracle.

"Not a worm." I spit out a tooth I hadn't known I'd broken. "Human."

"*Noisy.*" Light bleeds through Ra's pinfeathers, pours from his eyes. I've got one shot before they take me apart again. I test my restraints: restrictive, but not prohibitive. Like all sensible creatures, the father gods assume I wouldn't tear myself apart for no reason.

"Yeah. Well." I sort through my vocabulary for a pithy phrase. "Fuck you."

Good enough.

Blood gouts as I wrench myself loose of my fetters, bringing my forearms together. Flesh and pain are the oldest currency, older even than despair. If it's as easy as Meng Po claims, this is where it ends.

If it isn't, I'm clinically fucked.

I let the pain billow and wander down its tributaries. Past the doors to the outside of reality, the gateways to hell, past where Nyarlathotep and its siblings spin in the aether, waltzing to the music of the blind idiot god. I take a right at the edge of natural law, detour through time, down through the ebb and glow of my torture, following my soul to where it sleets hopefully towards destruction.

And there I find the door back to where the others are and turn the knob.

"Dude," I announce to a startled Fitz. "You're up."

His mouth opens, surprise in the colour of his expression. But before I can pull him through, drag him back so he can turn the gods into threads, roads that go nowhere except where we say, the patriarchs of heaven take notice. They seize us, all of us, split us through entropy, and fill my brain up with their ringing voice.

We can give Minah back to you.

And just like that, she's there in the supine dark, hair lacquered and gleaming, stars in her eyes, her skin warm and brown like I'd never seen it. Minah, alive as I've only imagined her. Minah, dressed in the life we'd never had together: thirty-seven, maybe, if I'd had to guess, with silver in that inkfall hair, lines like love poetry along the country of her smile. She holds out her arms to me, and I open my mouth to say something, something, *anything*. But I choke.

What I want to tell her is everything. How, that first night after the gods paid in the peace she wanted, I'd cried in a bed that had never been warm in the first place. I blubbered like a child orphaned on his birthday. I cried like Judas when the dust had settled, and there was no one there and nothing left but his regret to carry, like the ghost of a kiss.

I want to tell her how I can't walk to the supermarket, can't hear the first chord of 'Highway to Heaven' without breaking down into a heap. I want to tell her how much it hurts. I want to hold her, and I want, I want, I want—

"We can give you the life you were owed."

What I say instead is:

"I'm sorry."

I close my hands over her face. I'm allowed this, at least. I can give myself this. Just this. A brief memory of her jaw cradled in the book of my palms, like her cheekbones are psalms and prophecies, like the look in her eyes is a wedding vow to be read aloud so our happily-ever-after could finally come true. I stare at her, open-mouthed, aching.

And I let go.

"She wanted to *die*, you assholes."

The lights go out.

Minah vanishes like a blown bulb, a pop of white and then emptiness again, rushing in with a hiss.

"You fucking assholes. You don't get it, do you? Her idea of a happy ending was never having to come back to this shitty plane of existence again. She wanted *out*." My voice cracks into a scream. "But you can't *get* that, can you? Because dying scares you more than anything else…"

Through the void, its depth chandeliered with whispers, I feel Fitz reach out, discorporate but still infused with that same furious will. He is knotworks and tangles of unprocessed fate, maybes made into a billion threads, the fringe on a celestial flamenco dancer's skirt, each of them weighted down with a bell that when rung sounds like Fitz snarling *fuck you* at the cosmos. Roads to nowhere, somewhere, everywhere and everywhen.

Epiphany is a supernova in this abyss, and I look up as it floods into whatever I have left of a soul, fills me with light, with heat like the end of a tail pipe shoved against my hip. I burn to cinders in the revelation, a tattered laugh shaking itself free.

"We were wrong," I tell Fitz, the father gods, that faint stupid hope that Minah is there somewhere looking on, loving me.

I should have said *I love you*. The first time she died, I only said goodbye.

"We were wrong. Tanis isn't the Door. *I* am."

Here's the problem about kings. They never evolved to think quick. Every monarch, from the lord of the meanest farm-plot to the master of Olympus itself, presides over a parliament of scapegoats and lovers, ministers and murderers. Every decision is made by consensus, even if none of them will profess to that, preferring instead the fiction that the head has no need for a body, or its belly and bowels. So, kings faced with a problem like an assassin named Maria, they freeze, and that half of a second is all I need to catch enough of Fitz to hiss my intent.

"Well, fuck." His voice from every direction, laughing, and then it is suddenly no effort at all. The end of everything, halted by the turn of a key in its lock.

*   *   *

THE ROAD FINDS them, every last god.

They turn to look for a place that isn't asphalt, but there is only highway wherever their eyes dart, open sky the colour of a coyote's bad eye, and the smell of tar and tobacco and something like salt, sharp enough to tear a hole through eternity. No matter what they do, how they run, transform into swans or serpents though they may, there is nowhere for them but through the door at the road's end.

Somewhere, up where a sun might let its light lean on the earth, there's a voice: Coyote, humming the song he taught us as we rode along the Oregon coast, green in our lungs, pure again. *No gods grow old, no sea will take them home.*

This isn't what I see. This isn't what they see either, not with their shining eyes. But it might as well be. Five-dimensional space allows for a dizzying amount of artistic license. Slowly, as the sound of Coyote's voice becomes the face of the dead trickster, grinning down on his murderers with all the love he can muster in the heart they'd calved from his skinny ribcage, the father gods let go.

One after another, Ra and Marduk, Odin and Cernunnos, Tengri, Zeus and Jupiter, those bickering twins; I can't imagine how many times they'd tried killing each other to be the one and only, they put their heads down and they let go. Like condemned men promenading to their hanging, they go, their bodies stooped, their hands entwined. Even gods know there's no such thing as forever.

"I told you, didn't I?" says Coyote, all at once the sun and a corpse and a long-haired man in Saint Laurents, black and white silk with a rumpled grey tie, a dainty cigarillo in his slim hand. He smiles at me. There is a hole where a heart should have been and it should have been gruesome, but it's beautiful instead: the wound is verdigrised, ridged with emeralds pale as cream. Inside, I think I can see entire palettes of reality in slow orbit, light glinting along the edges of possibilities. In one of them, there's a timeline where Minah and I are alive, and in love, and there are children and a rose garden, and I hope to God that Rupert knows how sweet his life is. "They're just scared little boys."

"I saw you die."

I'm standing next to Fitz—or at least, I am standing next to the idea of something like Fitz, the Chronicler clean-shaven for the first time I've known him, hair pomaded, clothes fresh. I blink and Fitz becomes a kid, gawky and gangly, hunched to keep his height from offending, and he is still the Road leading the father gods home, and I'm the Door on the other side of nothing.

"Yes? I said I would die, didn't I?" Coyote smirks

as he drags from his cigarillo. "Weren't the first time, won't be the last, or even the most remarkable."

"You made such a goddamned fuss about it—"

"Because death isn't pleasant even for people like us. Not permanent, but not pleasant. Hey, did I tell you about the time I died four times to marry a woman?"

"That seems a bit like partner abuse," says Fitz. I realise, with a jerk, why he looks like a boy: there's not a scar or a hint of track marks to be seen, skin innocent as the face still round with puppy fat, brown eyes big and almost guileless.

I wonder what I look like to him.

"Probably, probably." Smoke ribbons from Coyote's teeth, becoming faces, bas reliefs of the father gods, their features sagging with resignation. "But no one ever asks if it's *consensual* abuse. Maybe it was a game for us. Maybe I liked being hacked up, and maybe she liked me begging, tail between my legs, telling her yes, baby, I'll even let you kill me if you'd just let me crawl into your bed."

He yips a coarse, crazed laugh.

"Love's always like that. You know what I'm talking about, Rupert. It's a lot more bite and a lot less breast than advertised." Coyote jogs his eyebrows and winks one eye, black as his hair, black as the ink on a marriage contract.

I breathe out. The gods keep shambling down the road, down and in and through Fitz's fingers, knitted into light, into fleece from the golden ram, on and on and on until they have his wrists, his forearms manacled by their weight, and Fitz is standing knee-deep in the glow of the deconstructed divine. He looks up at me, metaphor and meaning spindled around his fingers, and I know it's my turn now.

Where do gods go when the world is done with them?

"Hey, would they really have done it?"

"Done what?" says Coyote.

"Would they really have brought Minah back? Given her to me as flesh and blood?"

"Every last strand of hair. And she'd have been the real deal, too. The father gods have the power to do things like that, you know?"

"And George?"

"I don't understand why the hell you'd want somebody else's demon baby—"

"Just answer the damn question for once."

"Yes. I don't know if he'd have been happy about it. He's two now and being raised by a nice French family down in Bordeaux. But they would have brought him back for you."

Where do we put them? History suggests we pare them from wonder, dissect and diminish and decipher the reasons we made them, undo the miracle of them, and laugh as we say, *Here, this was because we were afraid the sun will not return,* and, *Here, this was so we can pretend the dead go on.*

Except that isn't true.

Ashes to ashes, dust to fucking dust. Nothing is eternal.

"If it helps to know"—Coyote's voice becomes kind, and makes me think of summers that won't die, fields of dark honey going forever—"they would have remade her from the atoms of what had come apart. Piece by piece. Put her back together, put a mind in a body that only wanted to sleep. And Minah would have remembered all of it."

"Would she have hated me?"

"You know she isn't that kind of woman. But you would have hated you. Forever.

The world gyres into multitudes, crystalline, and if I twitch my wrist, reality will reset into a place where gods weren't anything but fairy tales: a universe arctic and rigorously impersonal. Which wouldn't be so bad, would it? What with the stellar job they've done of shepherding the species, their ineptitude, their *hunger*—

They hold out their hands to us, blessings in the bowls of their palms. Everything, anything, *anything* so long as we put breath to a name. Even now, contained in the doorway to nowhere, their bodies reduced to photons, the father gods will bargain.

We will give you Minah.

We will give you a childhood, a boyhood, a life silent and sweet.

We will give you a life long and painless, more grandchildren than you can count, Naree at your side for always, always.

We will give you the promotion you've coveted, the house you've dreamed of, the wishes you've paid into a thousand wells, the world for your children; don't you want them to always be happy?

Your grandfather's blood, seared from your lineage. Human, forever.

The Lamp blinks on, and Cason licks his tongue across his teeth: broad as a lie, antlered, bangs hanging over eyes that are just shadow. Only his teeth shine, pale and perfect. He flickers erratically between aspects. One moment, his father's son, the horned god in eternal silhouette. The other, the most incandescent of the heavenly hosts, twelve wings in endless orbit around a body of holy flame, eyes without number.

But when he answers, he isn't either of those things. He's just… *Cason*. Washed-out button-down, thinning hair, white trainers, khakis rolled mid-way up his calves. "No."

"No," says Fitz, jerkily.

And then Tanis leans forward and I feel the Knife's fingers coil around my wrist, and she pushes down, and the image flickers again. We are in her living room with its no-budget-all-love decor, its clean IKEA furniture, its honeyed lights, and Naree's voice floating from the nursery. I feel love choke in my lungs, and I know it is Tanis, thinking there is no way she's allowed to be so happy, that perfect is as easy as falling asleep, one finger clutched in a tiny, tiny hand.

"That's all they've ever wanted," Tanis whispers, feral. "To feel. To be. To experience something that isn't immortality, long and featureless and drab. So let's give it to them."

Cason crooks a lupine smile. "All the fucking and feasting they could ask for."

"Forever." Fitz doesn't smile, his face rictused. "Then they get to do it all over again. Like it's brand new. Over and over and over."

No, beg the gods of never having to ask, never having to wonder if today's the day when it all comes down, when the paycheque stops, when the tap runs dry, when the light winks shut and there is only dark. When someone calls to say a mother, a father, a lover, a child is dead, dying, lost, and we will do everything to bring them home.

No, beg the patron gods of those bastards who have never once listened when anyone else said no.

I look down at Tanis's hand on my wrist, pushing down, and we are in my kitchen in the ghouls' florid manor with its baroque horrors, its clean marble, its sepulchral air. Cason and Fitz stand as audience, passing a cigarette between them, and it's just us and a slab of meat on a worn cutting board. My knife sinks through red muscle, white bone. The gods crack apart, their immortality bared like fresh marrow.

"Yes," I say.

We will give them flesh. We will robe them in capillaries and dress them in calcium, bedeck them with a heart, a mouth, and lungs that will hurt when they scream. We will have them wear skin like a bridal veil, wed them to death. We will spoon forever from the pith of these gods, and we will sear it over a fire. Until it blackens. Until there are ashes. Until there is nothing left except dust blowing in the wind.

Tomorrow, the gods will wake up as we all have at some point: baptised in terror, bloody, meat like the rest of us poor bastards.

Just meat.

"THAT WAS REALLY slick."

Amanda doesn't *quite* look human anymore. Her silhouette shimmers and spits, static barely contained, its run-off corroding to silver. When she speaks, her voice is an echo, the feedback from a thousand unseen speakers.

"The hell happened to you?"

The world settles: grainy at first, until it attenuates into coherent shapes. Wherever we are, this isn't Oregon anymore. My breath burns white; it's cold here. Fuck, it's cold. Worse even than the damp chill of London, a cold that tunnels down to the grey marrow. Slightly inexplicably, I find myself offended. After saving the world, which I assume is what we've done, you'd at least expect a blanket and a hot cocoa, if not an outright parade.

"You look different."

"Power is constant," Amanda murmurs. She raises a lean hand to the air and as I watch, light spirals in her palm. "It had to go *somewhere*."

"Did you know this was going to happen?" Cason is almost human again, save for the shadow of antlers curving from his forehead. Unlike me, he seems resolutely oblivious to the temperature.

"Of course she did," says Fitz, teeth chattering. "She's fucking Wikipedia."

"You mean she's Wikipedia incarnate, or—" Although I know I am witness to the apotheosis of a being already too powerful to measure in words. But if I can't have the world celebrate what we've done, at least I can run my mouth.

"Not today, Rupert." says Amanda, no threat in her tone at all, nothing like warning save for the radiance leaking from her. "Definitely not today."

I raise both hands. "I'll stop if we can get a space heater. Where the fuck *are* we, anyway?"

"Iceland." says Cason, wonderment in his face as he chews on the inside of his cheek. "My second honeymoon was here. Why the hell are we in Iceland?"

"Also, I think I'm getting frostbite—*shit*." Fitz drops his roll-up, hands quivering too hard for anything like purchase. "We just saved the world, Amanda. What gives?"

"I suppose I needed a running start." Her smile is beatific, haloed in neon-green. Reality bends where Amanda stands, gazing rapturously out into the wasteland, and it almost hurts now to rest my eyes on her.

"You still haven't answered," Cason says, doggedly. "Did you know you'd get their power?"

"Oh. Yes," breathes the thing that was Amanda, the thing who's become the fulcrum of the world, the axis of creation. A song wafts unsolicited into the foreground of my thoughts. God is a girl now. I can only hope she'd be more compassionate than the fathers that preceded her, more forgiving of the wounded creatures made in their flawed image.

"Are you going to use it to get rid of the, uh, new gods attached to you, then?"

"I was thinking of it," she says. "But perhaps I'll just remold them. After all, there is no limit to what can be done now."

"And this is how we enabled the singularity. All hail our new robot overlords."

Something like a smile crooks in the light.

"Close enough," says Amanda.

EPILOGUE

I LOOK DOWN skeptically at my plate of curry katsu. "This isn't what we ordered."

"Come on. We both know that when you're in a country stingy with their protein, you complain. Be happy with what you're given."

"Yes, but I don't think I need so much breaded pork."

Veles see-saws his hand. "Need. Want. Which is more important?"

The nice thing about Europe is it has no reason to

be suspicious of hulking Slavic men eating ramen on a cold autumn day, what with the ease of travel in the European region. Veles might be mountainous in measurements, but Scotland, I've come to learn, has no shortage of men in the same category, although the locals have a tendency of sharing silhouettes with a fridge. Daintily, the god separates his chopsticks and fishes a slice of charsiu from the bowl.

"I'm not sure I *want* this much pork, either!"

"You think too much, Rupert. Always have." His admonishment is full of teeth. He can't help it. Werewolf cults tint the divine soul. "Just eat."

"It really is a matter of principle. When a menu says that something is served with steamed broccoli, it should come out with an actual portion of steamed broccoli." I spear the lonely green vegetable on my plate with a fork. Now and then, I find myself wondering how it all became so banal. We'd kicked down the foundations of Heaven and installed the data-ghost of the World Wide Web in its place. Such an act should have more monumental consequences. Yet here I am, staring at broccoli and arguing with my maitre d' as we survey the competition. "This is just *garnish*."

"Also steam broccoli."

"All I'm saying is that this is ridiculous. But if this is what the adversary is doing, we're going to have to keep up, I *guess*." I nibble on one of the cutlets. Not bad. The curry is meekly spiced, but otherwise functional: not watery, not overly salted, one-note, which isn't strictly a mark against its flavour. "You know, they're really good at frying things here."

I wasn't sure if I could love Edinburgh. Half because it was forced upon me: Amanda and Fitz, despite the fact they own penthouses in six countries, wouldn't let me pick my own new nationality. It was Scotland or nothing. Like it or stay pathetically destitute for a man of my age. Also, it is intrinsically difficult to present any sort of argument when one's still processing the idea that Amanda, despite her new omnipotence, had elected to keep Fitz's prolonged company. Neither of them will admit to any kind of romantic relationship, but I have my suspicions. And frankly, it seems appropriate: a strung-out prophet on the road to recovery and the impartial spirit of information. If those aren't holy icons for the new millennium, I don't know what is.

So, I let Amanda write me my backstory: birth certificate, credit cards, a college degree I'd barely earned, a few failed applications locked in the system of Le Cordon Bleu, a single award nomination somewhere foreign to suggest that there is substance behind what initial reviews have labelled 'brazen' and 'experimental.'

The restaurant, I admit, I wasn't expecting.

At best, I thought they'd give me a nest egg to ration while I set myself up as a line-cook somewhere mediocre. But there it was, in an alley branching from Prince's street, less than ideal but not prohibitively out of the way, a second-storey restaurant all of my own. A fixer-upper with black mould in the back room, a kitchen so archaic it deserved its own museum. But it came with rent so cheap, I didn't think twice.

Because more important than anything else, this place is mine.

I ran the first phase of the restaurant as a dinner club, specialising in Malaysian-Scottish fusion, and it was moderately successful: Edinburgh, I discover, thanks to its predilection for spiced offal, has a reasonably adventurous palate. But then the gods came to my door. Not the ones from the formalised pantheons, the ones canonised by mythology. But the forgotten ones, the YouTube manifestations, the ones still trying to find their way, learning as the world does the new words for hope and faith.

The God of Being Missing serves as security detail these days, keeping out stray apparitions. The God of Missing People is my sous chef, happy in the idea of each thing in its place. And Veles, I found on my own, luring him to Edinburgh with a decent insurance plan. No reason to leave an old dog out there to fend for himself.

Cason shows up once, his entire family in tow, to celebrate the opening of Ambrosia. Tanis and Naree come every year, when fall transforms the city into fire. I make sure we have an outrageously ornamented birthday cake for Bee each time.

"By the way, here is review of restaurant." Veles holds out the papers. "You should read."

"Is it that bad?"

"No." Veles noisily spoons broth into his mouth. "You see."

It is on the last page of the entertainment section, nestled amid breathless accounts of trips to the Isle of Skye and nostalgic essays about the Mediterranean, all likely written by middle-aged white women of certain material standing who get together to expense a brunch every Saturday. The article isn't long, but there's a *picture* of me, standing at the top of the stairwell up to the restaurant, trying my hardest to look debonair. In the background, Veles, rolling his eyes at the camera.

I scan the review. *Ambrosia*, it writes and I try again to picture who the undercover critic could have been, whether it was the pencil-thin woman with a fur coat, or the man who lingered from morning to closing time, pecking at the daily rotations, *does not appear like much, at first glance, the refurbishment efforts clearly knee-capped by an uncooperative budget.*

Ouch.

But if you're willing to put aside the lacklustre furnishings and the uneven service (the head waiter, Veles, is frighteningly enthusiastic and possibly prescient, in a very real Twilight Zone *way), you'll find yourself treated to food befitting the ambitious name. Ambrosia is divine, if dangerously in love with spices...*

I skim the criticism of the food.

...Overall, however, I recommend this new rising star in the neighbourhood. Ambrosia will go far. And honestly, I'd die happy if this was my last supper before Ragnarök.

And that, ang moh, is how you end a story.

ACKNOWLEDGEMENTS

I LIKE THE IDEA of happy endings for urban fantasy heroes. I can't imagine what it's like: not only being told you have to save the world repeatedly, but having to repeatedly choke down all of your trauma because you're not supposed to talk about it. So, these guys get to have a happy ending. Just because.

And also because I've murdered Rupert Wong so many times now, it's getting a little ridiculous.

They say you'll always remember your first and I guess that's true. Rupert was my first entry into fiction; he was the first character I'd ever written with the intention of placing in a book. At least as an adult. And I will always love him for that reason. Guilt aside, it's why he's now running a little restaurant in my favorite European city. It'll be years before I can finally settle down in Edinburgh, but at least Rupert will live in her heart for me.

To everyone who has stayed with me throughout this ride, thank you. There may be prequels in the future, I don't know. We'll see. But either way, I hope y'all enjoyed yourselves.

To my mouse, thank you for listening to me wail about Rupert for years and years and years.

To my editor again, thank you for believing in me. You were the first person to give me faith that I could do this writing thing, and you were there for me as my friend through some of the worst years of my life.

To my guard puppy, thank you for being the heart of this book in some ways. *The Last Supper Before Ragnarok* is about love, about how love's the reason we fight, about where love will take us. Thank you for reminding me of that.

ABOUT THE AUTHOR

Cassandra Khaw is a scriptwriter in Ubisoft Montreal. Her work can be found in *F&SF*, *Lightspeed*, *Tor.com* and *Strange Horizons*. She has also contributed to titles like *Sunless Skies*, *Fallen London*, *Wasteland 3*, and *She Remembered Caterpillars*, which won the German Game Award for Best Children's Game. *Hammers on Bone*, her first novella, was nominated for the Locus Award and the British Fantasy Award. Her most recent novel *Food of the Gods* was nominated for the Locus Award.

FIND US ONLINE!

www.rebellionpublishing.com

/rebellionpub /rebellionpublishing /rebellionpub

SIGN UP TO OUR NEWSLETTER!

rebellionpublishing.com/sign-up

YOUR REVIEWS MATTER!

Enjoy this book? Got something to say?

Leave a review on Amazon, GoodReads or with your
favourite bookseller and let the world know!